The Brannigan Boys

When ex-Texas Ranger Joe Brannigan and his former partner, Seth Barnes, are murdered on Joe's ranch in New Mexico territory by unknown assailants, the rancher's three teenage sons, Danny, Jack and Jimmy, set out to find the killers and deliver them to the law.

Having established the identity of the murderers the three avengers continue their search only to find that the assassins have joined forces with a bigger gang of outlaws led by Casey Brown.

Can these three raw yet courageous teenagers possibly succeed in what threatens to be a suicidal mission? What chance have they against two gangs of hardened criminals?

The Brannigan Boys

ALAN IRWIN

A Black Horse Western

ROBERT HALE · LONDON

ISBN 0 7090 7356 9

Robert Hale Limited
Clerkenwell House
Clerkenwell Green
London EC1R 0HT

To Frank Barnes
for his unfailing support

Typeset by
Derek Doyle & Associates, Liverpool.
Printed and bound in Great Britain by
Antony Rowe Limited, Wiltshire

ONE

The three Brannigan brothers, returning from a visit to Doloro, four miles to the south, rode up to the house on the small Lazy B Ranch, located in the north-east of New Mexico Territory, close to the border with the Texas Panhandle. It was just before noon.

They dismounted, and led by Danny who, at eighteen, was the eldest of three sons who had been born in quick succession, they walked into the house. Danny was tall and broad-shouldered, like his father Joe Brannigan, with the same square chin and even disposition.

The elder of his two brothers was Jack, aged seventeen, a slim boy, almost as tall as Danny, with his mother's fair hair and blue eyes.

Jimmy, the youngest of the three, was barely sixteen. He was a wiry boy, of a normally cheerful disposition, who favoured neither of his parents.

The boys' childhood had been spent in Amarillo in the Texas Panhandle, where they had received their schooling. Joe Brannigan, a Texas Ranger, had been stationed at Amarillo, where he met and married his wife Ellen.

She was a strong woman, devoted to her husband and later to her three children. Tragically, she had died in a cholera epidemic two years previously and Joe, devastated by the loss of his wife, had decided to move north with his boys and try his hand at cattle ranching. He and his three sons had quickly learnt the rudiments of the cattle-raising business, and the boys were now accomplished cattle hands.

As well as his sons, Joe took with him to the ranch a close friend and ex-partner, Seth Barnes, who had saved his life when the two of them were chasing some cattle rustlers south of the Panhandle. Seth himself had been so badly crippled during the operation that he had been forced to quit his job with the Rangers.

Inside the Lazy B ranch house, Danny stopped short as he entered the living-room, with his brothers close behind him. Joe Brannigan was seated on an armchair, facing them. His head was slumped forward, his chin resting on his chest. There was a bullet-hole in the centre of his forehead and blood on his face.

Danny ran up to the armchair, followed by his brothers. Their father was obviously dead. Badly shaken, they stared at him in disbelief. Then Danny spoke.

'You two stay here,' he said. 'I'm going to check up on Seth.'

He found his father's friend in the small cabin that had been built for him near the house. He was lying on the floor, close to an overturned chair. Like Joe Brannigan, he had been shot in the head. Like Joe, he was dead.

Danny took a grip on himself and ran back to the house with the news. Distressed, the brothers were silent for a few moments. Joe had been a good parent, and there had been a close bond of affection between him and his sons. And Seth had long ago come to be regarded as a member of the family.

Danny spoke.

'Jack,' he said, 'you and Jimmy stay here, while I ride into town to get the undertaker to come out here for Pa and Seth. While I'm there I'll find out if anybody's seen any strangers around.'

He collected two blankets and placed one over his father and the other over Seth. Then he spoke to Jimmy.

'Before I go, Jimmy,' he said, 'have a good look at all the traces left behind by whoever it was that done this.' He picked on Jimmy for this task because the boy, who had ambitions to become a lawman, had taken a keen interest in the reading of signs which indicated the passage of humans on foot, horses, and various other animals.

Accordingly, Jimmy had prevailed on Seth, whose legendary skill in tracking down criminals had proved to be of considerable help to him as a Ranger, to pass on the fruits of his long experience of tracking and stalking an enemy. Seth had spent many hours with Jimmy, doing just this.

When Jimmy had completed a close examination of the area in and around the house, he was sure that three riders had visited the Lazy B since he and his brothers had left for town earlier in the day. They had ridden in from the south-east and had departed in the same direction.

One man had visited the house, another Seth's cabin, and a third, whose footprints were much smaller than those of the other two, had gone inside the barn. There was evidence that the house and cabin had been thoroughly searched, probably for valuables and cash.

Inside the barn, under a nailed-down floorboard in a corner of the loft, Jimmy found that the small box containing his father's savings, close on $800 in banknotes, was still in place, and had not been disturbed. He went back to his brothers and told them what he had found.

It was then, looking through their father's pockets, that they discovered that the handsome silver hunter timepiece that Joe's wife had given him not long before she died, had disappeared.

'I'm going into town now,' said Danny. 'When I get back we'll talk about what we're going to do, now that Pa's gone.'

When Danny reached Doloro, his first call was at the livery stable. He went inside to see the liveryman Dave Saxon, who had become a close friend of the family after Joe Brannigan had established the Lazy B Ranch nearby.

Saxon, a short stocky man in his fifties, was clearly

shocked when Danny told him of the deaths of the rancher and Seth Barnes.

'You any idea who did the shooting?' he asked Danny.

Danny shook his head. 'We figure the killings were done by three men,' he said. 'We don't know who they were. Have you seen any strangers around here lately?'

'No, I ain't,' Saxon replied.

'Well,' said Danny, 'as soon as I've seen the undertaker about burying Pa and Seth, I'll ask around town whether any strangers have been seen. I aim to get on the trail of those killers just as soon as I can.'

Saxon stared at him. 'That would be a dangerous job for a youngster like you to take on, Danny,' he said. 'Maybe you'd better leave it to the law.'

'The nearest lawman's a long way from here,' said Danny, 'and by the time he got here I reckon the trail of those killers would be plumb cold.'

'What about Jack and Jimmy?' asked Saxon.

'I'm going to have a talk with them about it when I get back,' Danny replied.

'All right,' said Saxon. 'I'll go with the undertaker when he rides out on his buckboard for the bodies. Then you can tell me what you've decided to do.'

Danny left the liveryman and went to see Jesse Randle, the blacksmith who doubled as undertaker. Shocked at the news, Randle said he would arrange for the burials to take place on the following day, on the top of a mound on the Lazy B, visible from the ranch house. Joe's wife Ellen had been buried at the same spot two years previously.

Danny parted from Randle and made some enquiries around town. Nobody had seen strangers in the vicinity recently. When he got back to the ranch his brothers met him outside the house. He told them about the arrangements he had made for the burials to take place on the following day. He could see that, although obviously upset, they were bearing up well.

'What I'm going to do as soon as we've buried Pa and Seth,' said Danny, 'is find those killers. I want you two to stay here while I'm gone, and keep this ranch running. Maybe we can hire some help.'

'I'm going with you,' said Jack. 'You can't do this on your own.'

'Me too,' said Jimmy. 'I want to catch those murderers just as much as you do, and I can help you to follow their trail.'

Danny studied the faces of his two brothers closely. He knew them well enough to decide that it would be useless to argue with them.

'All right,' he said. 'In that case, we'll either have to sell the cattle off, or get somebody in to look after them. There's no knowing how long we're likely to be away.'

When Randle and a helper arrived some time later to collect the bodies, Saxon was riding by the buck-board. He stayed until Randle left, then sat with the brothers in the living-room.

Danny told him that all three of them would be riding off in search of the killers as soon as they could get away.

'I still think,' said Saxon, 'that it's a purty dangerous job you're taking on, but I can see it ain't no
good me trying to change your minds. What about
the ranch?'

'We've been talking about that,' said Danny. 'We
can't think of anybody who might look after the herd
while we're away. We reckon we'll have to sell the
cows. I'm going to ask around after the burial tomorrow morning, to see if anybody's interested. Maybe
the bank manager can help us find a buyer.'

The burial took place at noon the following day.
As well as the boys, a number of townspeople were
present, also a well-dressed bearded man in his
fifties, who was a stranger to the brothers. When
the ceremony was over this man walked over to
them.

'My name's Parker,' he said. 'Grant Parker. I own
the Circle Dot ranch south of here. I knew your
father from way back and I was figuring on riding
over sometime to meet up with him again. Then I
heard late yesterday from a cowpuncher riding south
that he'd been murdered.

'He was a Ranger at the time we met, and he
happened across me in some rough country about
fifteen miles south of Amarillo. My horse had
stepped in a hole and had broken a leg. It was lying
on top of me, trying to get up.

'I was in a bad way by the the time your father
turned up and shot the horse. I was badly crushed,
unconscious, and bleeding inside. Your father built a
travois and got me to a doctor in Amarillo who

11

managed to fix me up. The doctor told me that your father had saved my life. That's why I'm here today to pay my respects.'

'Thank you for coming,' said Danny. 'My father's talked about you having a big ranch south of here, but he never mentioned about meeting you when he was a Ranger.'

'What're you aiming to do, now that your father's gone?' asked Parker.

'Me and my two brothers here,' said Danny, 'are riding off after the killers as soon as we can sell the cattle. We don't know how long we're likely to be away, and there's nobody to look after the herd.'

Parker eyed the trio in front of him closely.

'You're dead set on doing this?' he asked.

They all nodded.

'In that case,' he said, 'there's no need for you to sell the cattle. I'll send three of my hands over to look after them till you get back. They can take over tomorrow morning if you like.'

'We're mighty obliged to you, Mr Parker,' said Danny. 'Of course, we'll pay them the going rate for the job.'

'I owe your father a lot,' said Parker. 'I'd take it kindly if you'd let me keep them on my own payroll. It's a chance for me to repay just a little of what I owe him. You'll be doing me a big favour if you agree.'

Danny hesitated for a moment, then nodded his head.

'If that's how you'd like it,' he said, 'we accept, with thanks. We'll wait till your men get here tomorrow morning. When we've showed them around, we'll leave and try to pick up the trail of the killers.'

'Right,' said Parker, 'I'll send my top hand Ike Bentley and two other hands Regan and Hartley. Bentley's a good man. With him running things here, you'll have no need to worry.'

TWO

The following morning, the Brannigan boys rose early, took breakfast, and while they were waiting for the arrival of the Circle Dot hands, discussed the mission on which they were about to embark.

'We'll take rifles and six-guns with us,' said Danny, 'and plenty of ammunition. And we'll take three horses best suited for the job we aim to do.'

Each of the brothers had their own Colt .45 Peacemaker and Winchester rifle, purchased for them by their father a while back, after the death of Ellen Brannigan.

Joe Brannigan, knowing that it would distress his wife to see her young sons familiarizing themselves with firearms, had not encouraged them to do so while she was still alive.

But he was a firm believer that everyone should equip themselves to fight for their rights, and that owning a weapon was an essential requirement in an environment which was spawning a growing band of robbers and murderers. Joe himself had shown considerable expertise in the handling of the Colt

.45 Peacemaker which was his favourite handgun, and he had given his three sons a thorough schooling in the use, both of this weapon, and also of the Winchester rifle. But he had always emphasized that only as a last resort, when no other measures could resolve a situation, should the firearms be used.

All three boys had become proficient in the use of the weapons, with Danny showing a particular talent, surpassing even that of his father, in the handling of the six-gun. On the other hand, keen-eyed Jack proved to be an outstanding rifle shot when using the Winchester .44 -.40, with its extra rear sight for greater accuracy, which his father had bought him.

Jimmy's passion was for horses and riding. Contrary to most cowhands, to whom the cowpony was merely a necessary tool for the job in hand, he had a genuine liking for the animals.

When Bentley arrived at the Lazy B with the other two Circle Dot hands he had news for Danny and his brothers. It seemed that when Parker had got back to his ranch the previous day, a hand had ridden in from a three-day stay out on the range.

The hand mentioned to the rancher that he had seen three men riding south during the late afternoon of the day of the killings on the Lazy B. He had been resting in the shade inside a small grove of trees, and although the trio had passed close by, they had not seen him.

Not liking the look of the passing riders, the hand had stayed out of sight. He described the man riding nearest to him as a big man, around six feet tall, with long black hair. He had a deeply scarred right cheek and was riding a big palomino.

The rider next to him looked like a half-breed Indian. He was of average height and build, and was riding a pinto. The third rider was partly hidden from view and the Circle Dot hand could only say that he was a short slim man, with nothing distinctive about him. He thought the man was riding a bay horse.

'Looks like they may be the men who murdered your father,' said Bentley.

'Could be,' said Danny. 'What we'll do is follow their horse tracks as far as we can from here and if we lose them we'll ride to the Circle Dot and go to the place where the three riders were seen. If we can see some horse-tracks there, I'm sure Jimmy can tell if they tally with the ones the killers left here. If they do, we'll do our best to follow the tracks on from there.'

They left an hour later, following the tracks, which were heading in a southerly direction, but lost them just over a mile south of the ranch house.

When they arrived at the Circle Dot they were greeted by Parker who sent for his hand Willis, the man who had seen the three strangers riding over the Circle Dot range. He told Willis to take the three brothers to the exact place where he had seen the three riders.

When they reached the grove in which Willis had been hiding, Jimmy found some clear horse-tracks a little to the south. He identified them as being identical with the tracks he had seen on the Lazy B on the day his father had been murdered.

Danny spoke to Willis.

'Thanks to you,' he said, 'we have a good description of two of the killers. We'll follow these tracks as far as we can.'

They parted company with the ranch hand and rode on to the south. Jimmy was able to follow the tracks until darkness fell. They camped out overnight and continued the pursuit the following morning, during the course of which the tracks angled across the border into the Texas Panhandle, then took a south-easterly direction. But around midday they lost the tracks and spent the afternoon in a fruitless effort to pick them up again.

As darkness was falling, they looked around for a place to camp for the night. Glancing to the south, Jack saw a distant glimmer of light. He drew the attention of the others to it.

'Could be a camp-fire,' said Danny. 'Might even be at the camp of the men we're after, though I figured they'd be a lot further south by now. We'll move in closer, and Jimmy can sneak up and take a look.'

They waited a while until it was properly dark, then rode on to a point about four hundred yards from the light.

'It sure looks like a camp-fire,' said Jimmy. 'You two stay here while I go ahead on foot and take a look.'

Leaving his brothers behind, Jimmy headed cautiously for the light. Soon he could identify it as a camp-fire located in a small clearing on a flat stretch of ground studded with large boulders. Seated near the fire were three men, each holding a mug of

18

coffee in his hands.

Exercising the skills imparted to him by Seth Barnes, and using the boulders as cover, Jimmy silently moved to a position behind a boulder which was close enough to the fire to give him a good look at the three men. They were all slimly-built and slightly below average height. None of them was a half-breed. It seemed clear that they were not the men that he and his brothers were after.

Jimmy decided that his best plan would be to retire without the men becoming aware of his presence. He was just about to do this when he heard the sound of a cough from the far side of the boulder behind which he was hiding.

For a few moments he froze, then, when the sound was not repeated, he peered round the boulder. In the dim light from the fire, he could see a pair of legs stretched out on the ground, tightly bound together. Craning his neck still further, he saw a man, with his hands also bound, sitting with his back to the boulder.

Jimmy quickly withdrew out of sight as he saw one of the men by the fire get to his feet and start walking towards the bound man. He stopped in front of the prisoner and spoke to him. His voice, harsh and threatening, was clearly heard by Jimmy.

'Thought you'd like to know, Carter,' the man said, 'just what we're aiming to do with you. We're mighty tired of being chased around by you Rangers, and you're the one that's given us the most trouble. We knew you were following us, so we set a trap for you, and you sure fell right into it. You ain't never going to be able to come after us again. This is the end of the road for you, Carter.'

'You're crazy, Farrell,' said Carter. 'You know if you kill me, my friends in the Rangers ain't going to rest till you and your men are captured or killed.'

'We've thought of that,' said Farrell, 'and we've come up with a plan to make it look like your death was an accident. You know that deep canyon just south of here. Come daylight tomorrow, we're going to push you and your horse off the top of the canyon wall, then use a stick of dynamite to make it look like the ground gave way there when you were riding over it. What d'you think of the idea?'

Carter made no reply and Farrell, grinning broadly, returned to his companions by the fire.

Jimmy returned to his brothers to let them know that the men in the camp were not the ones they were chasing. Then he told them about the prisoner, and the fate in store for him the following morning.

'We can't walk away from this,' said Danny. 'The prisoner they're holding there is a Ranger. Maybe somebody Pa worked with. We've got to help him.'

Jack and Jimmy both nodded.

'You got a plan, Danny?' asked Jack.

'I've got an idea,' Danny replied. 'Let's talk about it. We can't do anything till they're bedded down. Then we'll see if they've posted a guard.'

The three brothers discussed Danny's plan for a while. Then they had a meal and rested till just after midnight, when they cautiously approached the position from which Jimmy had earlier spied on the three men by the camp-fire. Jimmy was carrying a coiled lariat in his hand. They stood behind the boulder, and looked towards the fire.

Two of the men were lying motionless on the ground, not far from the fire. Each was covered by a blanket. The third man was seated to the right of the fire, with his back to a boulder. He was smoking a cigarette. Jimmy recognized him as the man Farrell, who had earlier been telling Carter of his impending fate.

The prisoner was still sitting on the ground with his back to the boulder behind which Danny and his brothers were hiding.

Danny beckoned to his companions, and the three of them retreated, then worked their way round to a position behind a boulder not far away from the one against which Farrell was sitting. On the way they passed close to four picketed horses.

They watched as Farrell finished his cigarette, threw the end away, and leaned back against the boulder. He was wearing a six-gun and his rifle lay on the ground beside him. After a while his head nodded several times, then slumped forward, with his chin resting on his chest. A gentle snore came from between his lips.

Danny looked across at the two men by the fire. Both were lying motionless and appeared to be sleeping soundly. Softly, he ran up to the guard, followed by his brothers. He locked his arm around Farrell's throat to prevent him calling cut, and dragged him behind the boulder, out of the view of the two sleeping men.

While Jimmy watched Farrell's two companions,

Jack stuffed a gag into the guard's mouth and held it in place with a bandanna tied around his head. Then, with Danny still holding Farrell tight, Jack securely bound the guard's hands and feet.

Danny released his grip and dragged Farrell into the darkness well back from the fire, out of view of his companions, who were still sleeping soundly. The proceedings had been watched with interest by Ranger Carter who, understandably, had been unable to sleep.

Danny and his brothers moved quietly over to Carter and quickly removed the ropes from his arms and legs. They all moved behind the boulder while the Ranger flexed his limbs for a while. Danny handed him the six-gun he had taken from Farrell.

Then all four of them ran up to the two sleeping men near the fire. Danny and Carter jammed the muzzles of their six-guns against the chests of the two men and prodded them awake. Jack and Jimmy took the men's weapons.

Shortly after, when all three prisoners, hands and feet bound, were lying on the ground near the fire, Carter spoke to Danny and his brothers.

'I sure am obliged to you three,' he said. 'My name's Carter. I'm a Texas Ranger. There ain't no doubt you saved my hide. That's the Farrell gang over there. They were aiming to finish me off in the morning. Or maybe you knew that already?'

'We did,' said Danny. 'Jimmy here heard Farrell talking to you last evening.'

'I've been trailing the gang for three days,' said Carter. 'Had a partner with me, but he took sick a couple of days ago, and I left him with a doctor in Penroe. The gang jumped me yesterday when I wasn't expecting it.

'Farrell and his men held up a stagecoach south of Amarillo three days ago and killed the driver and one passenger. I aim to take them back to Amarillo for trial. How come you three happen to be in these parts?'

'I'm Danny Brannigan,' said Danny, 'and these are my brothers Jack and Jimmy. I'm wondering if you ever met our father Joe Brannigan. He was a Texas Ranger working out of Amarillo?'

'I sure did,' Carter replied. 'Up until a year ago I was operating in South Texas, but I did meet up with him, a couple of times. He was something of a legend in the Rangers. I heard he'd set up as a rancher in New Mexico Territory.'

'That's right,' said Danny, grimly, and went on to tell Carter of the murder of his father and Seth, and of the pursuit, by him and his brothers, of the killers.

'I'm mighty sorry to hear about your father,' said Carter. 'I can't say I recognize your description of the men who killed him. You say you've lost their trail?'

'That's right,' Danny replied. 'Around midday yesterday. We figured on riding further south today, hoping that we'd pick it up again.'

'I've just had an idea,' said Carter. 'Why not come back with me to Ranger headquarters in Amarillo? I could do with some help getting these three outlaws there, and maybe somebody there will recognize your description of those two men. You could watch out for any sign of them on the way, and enquire if anybody's seen them.

'And there's another thing. Did it strike you that maybe the three killers are men that your father had sent to prison? Maybe it was a revenge killing. When we get to Amarillo we can look up the records of your father's arrests and see if any of the men he sent to prison have been set free recently.'

'From what you say,' said Danny, 'I reckon we should go with you. We're ready to leave when you are.'

They rested for a few hours and left at daylight with the three prisoners, hands bound, riding their own horses. They reached Amarillo without incident, late in the evening of the same day. During their journey, they had received no reports of possible sightings of the killers of Joe Brannigan, and Jimmy had seen no sign of the tracks of their horses.

After the prisoners had been jailed, Danny and his brothers, before parting with Carter to book in at a hotel, arranged to meet him at the office of Captain Ford of the Texas Rangers the following morning.

THREE

When Danny and the others went into Ford's office after breakfasting in the hotel dining-room, Carter was already there with the captain. Ford was a tall, lean, decisive-looking man in his fifties. The boys recollected meeting him a few times when the family was living in Amarillo.

'Ranger Carter,' said the captain, 'has just told me about your father. I'm mighty sorry about what's happened to him. He was a fine Ranger and a good friend of mine. We'll do anything we can to help you find his killers.

'Ranger Carter also told me about you saving his hide, and we're mighty grateful for that. The way you three got the better of the Farrell gang, it looks like you boys are taking after your father.

'Now if you can give me the descriptions of two of the killers maybe I can bring them to mind. I reckon it's possible your father tangled with them in the past.'

Danny repeated the descriptions given by Willis, the Circle Dot hand, of two of the three men riding across Circle Dot range on the day of the killings.

Ford leaned back in his chair, staring up at the ceiling, his brow furrowed in thought. Danny and the others waited in silence. Suddenly the captain sat upright and looked at them.

'It could be the Taylor gang,' he said. 'They ain't been around for a long time. The leader Rod Taylor was a big man with long black hair and a scarred face, and one of his men was a half-breed Indian called Chako.

'As far as I can recollect they were captured after a stagecoach robbery. Your father was leading a posse that trailed them to a hideout they were using at the time. Let me look in the files. There's bound to be something in there about the gang.'

He got up and walked to the door of a big cupboard behind him. Its shelves were stacked with papers. He sorted through these for a while, then turned with several sheets of paper in his hand.

'Got it!' he said, and sat down to read through the papers. Then he looked up at the others.

'From what it says here,' he told them, 'Farrell and his men were called on to surrender, but they decided to shoot it out with the posse. There were four men in the gang, and one of them, who was shot by your father and died on the spot, was Taylor's kid brother Frank.

'The other three were Rod Taylor, Chako, and a man called Wilson. They were all taken alive. There were no casualties on our side. The robbers were tried here in Amarillo and they were all sentenced to eight years in the penitentiary.'

He looked through the papers for the date of the trial, then continued.

'Which means that they would probably be released some time around now. What I'll do is telegraph the penitentiary right now and see if they've been freed. Should get an answer by tomorrow. You'd better hang around till it comes through. If they were free when your father was killed, it could be that they were the ones responsible for his death.'

'We'll stay till that reply comes through,' said Danny.

'Good,' said Ford. 'I'll let you know when it arrives. I know you're set on finding the killers yourselves, and I know it ain't no good me trying to change your minds. But remember, if you do happen to locate them in Texas after you leave here, contact us right away and we'll send men to take them into custody.

'I'd better give you a letter explaining who you are, and what the situation is. If you need help from us, show it to the nearest Ranger.'

It was just before noon on the following day when the brothers received a message that Ford wanted to see them. As they entered his office he picked up a file of papers lying on the desk in front of him.

'I've got the answer,' he said. 'All three men – that's Taylor, Chako and Wilson – were released just under three weeks ago. Nobody at the penitentiary knows where they were going.'

He handed Danny a copy of an old Wanted poster

bearing pictures of the four men, including Frank Taylor, now dead.

'As to where they are now,' he went on, 'I just had a thought.'

He looked through the file until he found the entry he wanted.

'This might help,' he said. 'Eight years ago, Reuben and Mary Taylor, the parents of Rod and Frank, were running a farm about a hundred and sixty miles south of here, not far from the Colorado River, and near a small town called Trask. I don't know if they're still there, but in case they are, and you don't find any trace of the gang soon, it might be a good idea for you to ride down there. Maybe they've been seen in the area.'

'We'll do that,' said Danny, 'and we're obliged for your help.'

They left an hour later, heading in a southerly direction, and enquiring of the few people they encountered as they rode along, whether there had been any sightings of the Taylor gang. But they were disappointed.

They camped out overnight, and on the following day they rode on in the direction of Trask. They saw no one until, in the early afternoon, they rode into the small town of Brody, where they bought some provisions and established that nobody there had seen the Taylor gang.

They continued south, and had covered about five miles when Danny breasted a rise ahead of his brothers and saw a group of three men a short distance ahead. They were standing by a group of cottonwood trees close to a narrow stream. Another man was lying on the ground close by.

Beyond the cottonwoods the stream turned and ran close to the foot of the rise on which Danny's horse was standing. Something about the group sounded a note of warning to Danny and, motioning to his brothers to halt, he retreated before he was seen by anyone below. They all dismounted and crawled up to some rocks scattered along the top of the rise. Using these as cover they watched the men down below.

Almost immediately, their attention was drawn to a herd of sheep on the far side of the group of men. Looking back at the men by the tree, they saw that the man on the ground had the loop of a lariat round his body, under the arms, the other end of the rope being tied to the pommel of the saddle on one of the horses.

It looked as though the man had been dragged over the ground to the spot where, moving feebly, he was now lying. He was a swarthy man, roughly dressed, wearing a long coat. As he lay there, one of the three men standing nearby walked up to him, bent down, and started to remove the loop of rope from around his body.

Then he hurriedly stepped backwards as one of the three border collies which were accompanying the herd ran up and leapt at him. He fended off the dog with his left hand, drew his revolver, and shot it through the head.

The watchers heard the faint sound of the shout of anguished protest coming from Juan Alvarez, the

29

Mexican sheepherder. Ignoring him, the man finished removing the rope from around the body of the prisoner, pulled him to his feet, and tied his hands behind him with a short length of rope, taken from his pocket.

Leaving the prisoner standing where he was, the man walked up to the cottonwood, carrying the lariat, and threw one end over a high branch. Then he started a conversation with his two companions.

'It's a hanging party,' said Danny. 'I reckon they're fixing to string that herder up. You remember Pa told us about some ranchers who're set on stopping any sheep from crossing public land that the ranchers are using to raise their cattle. And they ain't got no right to do that.'

'What can we do?' asked Jack.

'We've got to do what Pa would have done,' Danny replied. 'We've got to stop them. I wouldn't rest easy if we rode on and left that man to die. Are you with me?'

Both his brothers nodded. 'What's the plan?' Jack asked.

'Whatever we do, we'd better do it fast, said Danny. 'I figure they're aiming to string that herder up any time now.'

After Danny had hurriedly explained his plan, Jack and Jimmy, carrying their rifles and six-guns, ran along the side of the rise, out of sight of the group below.

At the same time, Danny ran to his horse, mounted it, then rode over the top of the rise and down the slope towards the group standing near the cottonwood. He saw that one of the men was now holding a horse in position under the tree, and two others were just about to hoist the sheepherder into the saddle.

On catching sight of the approaching rider, the two men released their captive and pushed him to one side. Then all three stood facing Danny, awaiting his arrival. When he reined in his horse a few yards in front of them, one of the men spoke.

He was a big man, thickset and bearded, wearing clothes of rather better quality than his companions. His name was Warner, owner of the small Bar 10 cattle ranch on whose range he was now standing. The men with him were two of his hands, Bellamy and Bradley. Each one of the three was wearing a six-gun.

'This is Bar 10 range,' said Warner, eyeing Danny closely. 'You got business here?'

'I didn't have,' Danny replied, forcing himself to stay calm, 'until I spotted what was going on down here. It looked to me like you was aiming to hang this herder.'

'It ain't no business of yours what we do,' said Warner, 'but you're right. I'm Warner, owner of this ranch, and we're going to hang this man and kill his sheep. I want all this grass for my cows. I don't want any sheep passing over my range. Where sheep have been, cows won't graze.'

'This is public land,' said Danny. 'This herder has the right to take his sheep across it.'

Warner's face reddened. 'You'd better watch your mouth,' he said. 'Nobody who's still wet behind the ears is going to teach me *my* business. Any more lip from you and you're liable to be getting the same treatment as this herder.'

Looking beyond the men facing him, Danny caught a glimpse of his brothers moving through the cottonwoods towards the backs of Warner and his men.

'I ain't going to let you hang this man,' said Danny. 'It'd be plain murder. The wise thing for you to do would be to leave him here with me, and go about your business.'

Warner lost his temper and reached for his gun, determined to cut the interfering young stranger down to size. But the gun fell from his hand and he jerked backwards as the bullet from Danny's Peacemaker drilled into his right shoulder.

Warner's two cowhands started to reach for their pistols, then stopped abruptly as two rifle shots sounded close behind them in quick succession, and first Bellamy's, then Bradley's, high-crowned hat was jerked from its owner's head by a rifle bullet.

Danny covered the three men with his revolver as his brothers relieved Bellamy and Bradley of their six-guns, walked out from behind them, and stood by Danny's side. Danny was shaken by his first participation in a gun duel, but he knew that his shooting of Warner had been unavoidable. He congratulated Jack on his marksmanship.

'You perforating their headgear like that sure got their attention,' he said.

Danny handed Jimmy his knife. 'Cut the herder free, Jimmy,' he said.

When this had been done, the Brannigan boys and the herder stood side by side, facing the rancher and his men.

'That was a fool thing you did, Warner,' said Danny. 'Look at the trouble it's got you into. All you had to do was let these sheep cross your range, which they've every right to do.

'Now let me tell you what we're aiming to do. Our father was a Texas Ranger, and a good friend of Ranger Captain Ford at Amarillo. It so happens we saw Captain Ford early yesterday.

'I'm going to ride back to Brody now. I noticed they have a telegraph office there. I'm going to send Captain Ford a message telling him just what's happened here today. And I'll tell him to expect another message as soon as me and my brothers have helped the herder to take his sheep clear across your range to the other side of your boundary.

'If he doesn't get that second message, he's sure going to look into the reason why. When I get back from Brody you and your men'll be free to go. Meanwhile, maybe they'll have a look at your shoulder.'

Danny turned to his brothers.

'Keep them well covered till I get back,' he said, before leading the sheepherder out of earshot of Warner and his men. 'You are all right?' he asked him.

'I am all right, *señor*,' replied the herder, 'except for some cuts and bruises. My name is Juan Alvarez. I think that I owe you my life.'

'I'm Danny Brannigan,' said Danny, 'and with me

are my brothers Jack and Jimmy. Where are you aiming to take those sheep?'

'To mountain pasture in New Mexico Territory, *señor*,' the herder replied.

'How soon can you take them over the eastern end of the Bar 10 range?' asked Danny.

'Before dark tomorrow, *señor*,' Alvarez replied.

'Good,' said Danny. 'Maybe you can get them started now. We'll catch up with you later.'

'I will do that, *señor*,' said Alvarez, 'as soon as I can bury my dog.'

Deeply grieved, he picked up the dead collie, and holding it in his arms, he walked towards the herd.

When Danny returned from Brody he noticed that Warner's shoulder had a rough bandage on it.

'You three can go now,' he told Warner, 'and remember what I said about the law.'

The brothers watched as Bellamy helped Warner up into the saddle. Then, without a word, the trio rode off in the direction of Brody, where Danny had noticed a DOCTOR sign on one of the houses.

About an hour before dark Danny and his brothers caught up with Alvarez and his flock, and shortly after this they reached an area which the herder selected as a bed-ground for the night. Here they made camp, and sat down for supper with Alvarez. The remaining two collies were close by.

'I thank you, *señores*, said the herder, 'for what you have done to save me and my herd.'

'We're glad we turned up at the right time,' said Danny. 'What Warner and his men were doing was

34

dead wrong. I don't reckon they'll trouble you again.'

'There are many ranchers like Warner,' said Alvarez. 'They believe that where sheep have grazed, cows will not go to eat. And they believe that sheep taint the waterholes so that cows will not drink there. But these things are not true.

'Also, they say that sheep are stupid animals, and this *is* true. They easily get trapped in bogs and streams; they wander off to feed in the night; and sometimes they take sick by eating too much.'

Interested in Alvarez's work as a sheepherder, the brothers discussed it with him for a while. Then Alvarez asked them where they were heading. Danny told him about the murder of their father and his friend, and about their pursuit of the killers.

'We think that maybe they were heading in this direction,' he said, 'but we ain't sure. We lost their tracks a while back. I don't suppose you've seen them?'

He handed the Wanted poster over to Alvarez, explaining that the pictures on it were taken ten years previously. The herder inspected the poster closely. Then he pointed to the pictures of Rod Taylor, Chako and Wilson.

'These men I leave seen, *señor*,' he said, 'and only three days ago. It was east of here. They rode into my camp after dark, and ordered me to cook a meal for them. I pretended that I knew no English and the half-breed spoke to me in Mexican.

'I was glad when they left, after they had eaten. I could see that they were bad *hombres*, *señores*, and I feared that they might kill me before they left.'

'Did you get any idea where they were going?' asked Danny.

'I heard them talking while they were eating,' Alvarez replied. 'I heard one of them say something about a farm near Trask, but I don't know if they were going there. When they left they were riding south.'

'They could have been heading for their parents' farm near Trask,' said Danny. 'I reckon we should ride there as soon as the herd has left Bar 10 range, and check whether they've been seen.'

They reached the boundary at dusk on the following day, and next morning the brothers took their leave of Alvarez and headed south towards Trask. In the early afternoon they stopped for a meal in the shade of a small copse, just off the trail and close to a rock outcrop, eighteen feet high, with gently sloping sides.

They had just finished the meal, and were preparing to leave, when they heard the sounds of distant gunfire coming from the north. They stood at the edge of the copse, looking in that direction.

A stagecoach, hauled by a team of six horses galloping at full stretch, was rapidly approaching them along the trail. The driver was urging his team on, and the shotgun rider by his side had turned in his seat and was returning the fire of five riders, who were coming up from behind, slowly gaining on the coach.

As the brothers watched, they saw one of the riders go down. Almost immediately after this, the shotgun rider jerked backwards and fell off his seat to the ground. A moment later, the driver slumped forward and rolled sideways off his seat to join his companion. The team continued to pull the coach onward at the same fast pace.

'Get mounted, Jimmy, ready to stop that team!' yelled Danny, 'but wait here till I give the word.'

Then he and Jack grabbed their rifles, ran to the outcrop, and quickly scrambled to the top. They lay down, facing the approaching riders, and immediately started firing at them. Danny missed twice before hitting a rider, but Jack, shooting with his usual precision, needed only three shots to bring the other three down.

The passengers inside the coach had seen the driver and shotgun rider as they were falling to the ground, and they looked apprehensively out of the coach windows at the four riders still in pursuit. They watched, incredulously, as one by one, the four went down.

As the last rider fell, Danny shouted down to his brother below.

'Go now, Jimmy!' he yelled.

Jimmy sprang into action and urged his mount after the coach, which had now passed abreast of the copse. Gradually, he gained on it, and as he raced alongside he waved at the passengers staring out at him. When he drew level with the lead horses he transferred from his own mount on to the back of one of these, then reached down for the reins. Gently, he reined the horse in and eventually the coach came to a halt.

Danny and Jack rode out to check the men on the ground. They found the driver and shotgun rider both dead. Of the riders who had been attempting to hold up the stage, one, who had been shot by the shotgun rider, was dead. The other four had gunshot wounds which were severe, but not, thought Danny, life-threatening. One of them had also suffered a broken leg when falling from his horse.

Danny and Jack collected all the weapons from the four wounded men, and tied their hands and feet. Then, leaving them lying where they were, they rode over to the stationary stagecoach.

Jimmy was standing close to it with the passengers, one woman and two men. One of the men was an elderly gambler, the other a drummer. The woman, Ruth Hutton, was the wife of Ben Hutton, the station agent at the stageline office in Trask. She was returning from a visit to relatives in Amarillo.

'Jimmy,' said Danny, 'round up the horses those men were riding.'

As Jimmy ran to his horse, Danny turned to the stagecoach passengers.

'The driver and shotgun rider are both dead,' he said, 'and so is one of the men who tried to hold you up. The others ain't in no state to cause any more trouble.'

He spoke to Ruth Hutton.

'Are you all right, ma'am?' he asked.

'I'm all right,' she replied, 'but I'm grieving for the two men who were on the box. They were both good friends of me and my husband. My husband is Ben Hutton. He's the station agent at the stageline office in Trask. There's a shipment of gold-dust in that strongbox. Maybe those robbers knew about it.'

'How far is it to Trask?' asked Danny.

'About eight miles, I reckon,' she replied.

'I've handled a team now and then,' said Danny. 'I figure I can drive the coach on to Trask. Then maybe your husband can send somebody out to pick up the dead men and the prisoners.'

'He'll do that,' she said, 'and I can tell you he's going to be mighty grateful to you and your friends for stopping this robbery.'

'They're my brothers Jack and Jimmy,' said Danny. 'I'm Danny Brannigan.'

Taking a good look at the brothers, Ruth Hutton felt surprised that such a youthful trio had managed to foil a robbery attempt by a band of hardened criminals. She turned, and climbed back into the coach. The other two passengers followed her.

Before climbing on to the box, Danny had a word with his brothers, and it was agreed that they would stay with the prisoners until help arrived from Trask.

FOUR

When the coach rolled into Trask a little over an hour later, Danny spotted the stageline office and brought the coach to a standstill outside it. Coming out of the office, Ben Hutton, startled at the sight of the unfamiliar driver and the absence of a second man on the box, ran to the door of the coach and looked inside for his wife.

Greatly relieved to see her there, he helped her down, and she told him of the attempted hold-up, the killing of the two men on the driver's box, and the intervention of Danny and his brothers.

Hutton turned to Danny, who had climbed down from the driver's box.

'The Company's going to be mighty grateful to you and your brothers when they hear about this,' he said. 'There's a valuable shipment in that strongbox. And I've got a feeling that the gang that attacked the coach is one that's been bothering us for a long time.

'I'll get a party organized to go out and bring those four prisoners and the three bodies back to town. I'll get the doctor to go along as well.'

41

'You can count me in as one of that party,' said Danny.

'All right,' said Hutton, 'and while you're away, I'll send a telegraph message to the Ranger headquarters in Amarillo asking them to pick up the prisoners as soon as they can.'

The party, taking a couple of buckboards with them, arrived at the scene of the attempted hold-up as darkness was falling. The doctor patched up the injured men and pronounced them capable of surviving the journey back to Trask. He reckoned they would all live to be hanged for murder.

When they reached Trask late in the evening, Hutton arranged accommodation and guards for the prisoners, and the undertaker collected the bodies of the three dead men. Hutton said that the law would pick up the prisoners in a few days' time.

Danny and his brothers stayed at the hotel overnight. As they were leaving it after breakfast, Hutton came out of his office and beckoned to them to come over. He led them inside and sat at his desk.

'Thought you'd like to know,' he said, 'that from some papers we found on the bodies, and information we got by telegraph, we're certain now that it was the Crawford gang that attacked the stage yesterday.

'It's the sort of operation they've been carrying out for three or four years now, and a reward's been offered for their capture. I reckon that reward'll be handed over to you three.'

Hutton went on to ask Danny about their plans for the immediate future. Danny told him about the killing of their father and their pursuit of Rod Taylor and his gang. He asked Hutton whether Taylor's father was still farming in the area.

'Yes, he is,' said Hutton, 'and three days ago, Rod Taylor and two men were seen at the homestead. We heard they'd been released from prison a while back. The next day I saw the three of them in town. They bought provisions and rode off towards the east, but I've no idea where they were heading.'

'We'll ride east ourselves, then,' said Danny, 'and Jimmy here'll try to pick up their trail.'

'Just a minute!' said Hutton. 'After the way you three dealt with the Crawford gang, I want to help you if I can. And I've just had an idea. Before Taylor and the others left, Taylor went into the telegraph office next door. Maybe the message he sent would give you some idea of where they're going.

'It so happens that the telegraph operator, Hiram Daley, is a good friend of mine. I reckon I could persuade him to let me know what was in that message, if he happens to remember. Wait here, and I'll go and have a word with him.'

Ten minutes later, Hutton returned.

'You're lucky,' he said. 'Hiram still had a copy of that message. I have it here.'

He handed a sheet of paper to Danny, who read it, then showed it to his brothers. It was addressed to 'Mark Delaney, Alamo Saloon, Fort Worth, Texas.' It read 'Accept proposition. Will contact you at Fort Worth about one week from today. Taylor.'

'Well,' said Danny, 'we know now where they were heading when they left here, and that's a big help. We're obliged to you and the telegraph operator, Mr

Hutton. We're leaving for Fort Worth now.'

He handed the message back to Hutton, who looked at it again.

'I'm wondering just what that proposition was,' he said.

'Me too,' said Danny. 'It wouldn't surprise me if it had to do with a criminal operation of some sort.'

The brothers arrived at Fort Worth five days later, in the evening, and took a room at the Murray Hotel, in the middle of town, opposite the Alamo saloon.

Next morning, after breakfast, they went to Ranger headquarters in town, and were shown into the office of Ranger Captain Bixby, a lean, alert-looking man in his early fifties. Danny showed Bixby the letter which Captain Ford had given him in Amarillo, and explained the reason for their presence in Fort Worth.

'I met your father only once,' said Bixby, 'but I've heard a lot about him. I'm sorry to hear about his death.'

'This man Delaney the telegram was sent to,' said Danny. 'I expect Taylor's been in contact with him by now. D'you know him?'

'I do,' Bixby replied. 'He owns the Alamo saloon. He's a big man, bearded, and in his forties, I'd say. Always dresses pretty smartly, with a black jacket and a fancy waistcoat.

'There's talk that some of the games he runs are crooked, but nothing's been proved yet. If the Taylor gang has been in touch with him, I'm just as curious as you are to find out what they were talking about.'

Danny produced the Wanted poster which carried

pictures of the Taylor gang and handed it to Bixby, who studied it closely.

'Can't say I've seen them in town,' he said. 'Maybe they're holed up somewhere nearby. Delaney has living-quarters over the saloon. One way in is through a door at the top of some steps on the outside of the building. Maybe he was visited there after dark by Taylor.'

'Maybe so,' said Danny. 'We'll stay in town for the time being. One of us'll keep watch from our hotel room window on the Alamo saloon opposite. We'll be watching for one or more of the Taylor gang to go in there. And at the same time we'll watch out for Delaney leaving and riding out of town. Maybe he'll lead us to the gang.'

'Right,' said Bixby. 'You do that. And let me know if anything interesting turns up, or if I can give you any help.'

'We will,' said Danny, and the three brothers left the Ranger Captain's office. On the boardwalk outside the hotel they paused to discuss the arrangements for sharing a continuous watch on the Alamo saloon from the hotel bedroom window. Then Jimmy went to the bedroom while the other two crossed the road.

Leaving Jack standing on the boardwalk outside the Alamo saloon Danny went inside and walked up to the bar, where the barkeep was busy serving a bunch of customers. With his back to the bar, Danny looked around. As he did so, a door opened at the far end of the saloon. A man emerged and walked down the saloon towards the swing doors.

The man fitted Bixby's description of Delaney, right down to the black jacket and fancy waistcoat. As he approached the doors he called out to the barkeep.

'Going to the bank,' he said. 'Back soon.'

'All right, Mr Delaney,' said the barkeep, who was still busy attending to the customers in front of him.

Danny walked out of the saloon to rejoin Jack.

'That was Delaney who just came out,' he said. 'You saw him?'

'Yes,' replied Jack. 'I figured it was him. What do we do now?'

'We wait and watch,' said Danny, 'and if Delaney leaves town we follow him.'

Their attention was caught by a horseman riding towards them from the south. Seeing Danny and Jack, the rider veered towards them and came to a stop in front of them. He was a rangy man, with a long weather-beaten face.

'Howdy,' he said. 'Name's Varney. I'm trail boss for an outfit that's trailing a herd of two and a half thousand Box K longhorns over the Chisholm Trail to Caldwell, Kansas. Two men quit during the night just before we reached the Red River, for a reason that ain't clear to me. And another one took a fall and busted his shoulder so bad he can't carry on.

'Right now, my men are holding the herd just south of Red River Station. That's where we're aiming to cross. The Red there's safe for fording just now. I've come back here to see if I can hire three hands to replace the ones I've lost. You interested in helping out? The job pays thirty dollars a month.'

'Sorry, Mr Varney,' said Danny. 'We've both got another job in hand just now. But I sure hope you find the men you need.'

Varney grunted, and rode on to the Alamo saloon, where he dismounted and went inside. A minute later, Delaney, returning from the bank, followed him in.

Jack and Danny joined their brother in the room at the hotel. Jimmy had seen Delaney leave the saloon and return, also the arrival of Varney. Danny told him about Varney's search for trail hands.

Joe Brannigan had told his sons about the Chisholm Trail, named after a Scotch-Cherokee trader, Jesse Chisholm, who, many years earlier, had opened up part of it as a wagon road, running roughly north and south, between South-Central Kansas and his trading post on the Canadian River.

Nowadays, from spring to autumn, hundreds of thousands of cows walked over the trail on their long journey from Texas to railheads in Kansas.

Some time later, Danny left the others and went across the street to the general store, to make a few purchases. He was standing at the counter while the storekeeper was searching for an item at the back of the store, when the door opened and Varney walked in. Recognizing Danny, he nodded.

'Any luck?' asked Danny.

'Not so far,' Varney replied. 'From what the saloon-owner told me, it looks like I'm going to have to make do with the hands I've got.'

A few minutes later, Danny left the store and

returned to the hotel room. Shortly after this, they saw Varney ride out of town. He was heading north.

Danny and Jack sat on their beds while Jimmy sat on a chair keeping watch through the window. They had been chatting together for twenty minutes when Jimmy suddenly stood up and called the others over. Delaney had come out of the saloon.

They watched as the saloon-owner walked a little way along the street, then turned into the livery stable where they themselves had stabled their horses the previous day. Five minutes later he came out, riding a big chestnut gelding, and headed south out of town.

'You stay here, Jimmy,' said Danny, 'and we'll follow Delaney. We'll take the field glasses. Watch out for Taylor and the others while we're away. And don't worry if we're missing for a few days.'

Jack and Danny went to the livery stable for their horses. Quickly, they saddled and mounted them, then rode along the street in the direction taken by Delaney. As they reached the outskirts of town they could see him in the distance, riding fast, and heading for a low ridge to the south.

They waited until he had ridden through a narrow gap in the ridge without a backward glance, and was hidden from view on the far side. Then they headed for the gap, rode cautiously through it, and stopped as soon as they had a good view of the ground ahead. They both scanned it carefully, but Delaney was not in sight.

Danny took the lead and soon picked up the tracks left by Delaney's horse. Leaving the gap, he had veered to the left and headed towards a small hill, with a circular base, which lay ahead. The tracks rounded the base of the hill, and continued in the same direction as before.

They followed Delaney for the next eight miles, several times sighting the distant rider. On the last occasion, watching through field glasses, they took cover as Danny saw Delaney halt at the entrance to a small ravine. Suddenly, a man appeared from behind a large boulder close to the entrance, and waved to Delaney.

The saloon-owner waved back and rode on into the ravine, disappearing from view. The look-out returned to his position behind the boulder.

'Looks like he ain't going no further, Jack,' said Danny. 'Maybe Taylor and the others are hiding out in that ravine. One thing's sure, we can't get any closer in daylight without that look-out seeing us. We'll stay here till after dark.'

They found a position from which they and their mounts would not be visible to Delaney if he returned to Fort Worth by the same route before darkness fell. Then they settled down to watch and wait.

There were still two hours to go before sunset when they saw the saloon-owner ride out of the ravine. He was not alone. They counted another ten men with him. As the riders drew closer, they were able to identify Taylor and, riding close to him, his men Chako and Wilson.

The other seven riders, strangers to Danny and Jack, were outlaw gang leader Casey Brown and his men. Brown, distantly related to Taylor, was a noted desperado who had collected a group of unscrupulous men around him intent on making money the easy way – by robbery in one form or another. He was a tall, broad man, with beetling eyebrows and a black beard.

The riders passed the two concealed watchers and came to a brief halt a quarter of a mile further on. Then Delaney and one of Brown's men, a half-breed called Butler, continued on towards Fort Worth, while the remaining riders headed off in a northerly direction.

'Wonder where Taylor and the others are going,' said Jack.

'I ain't got no idea,' said Danny. 'It looks like maybe Delaney's bought them some news that's triggered off some sort of operation. It wouldn't surprise me if those men riding off with Taylor and his friends turn out to be criminals.'

'What do we do now?' asked Jack.

'We'd better follow the ones heading north,' Danny replied. 'We don't want to lose Taylor and his men, now that we've finally located them. Let's follow them and see what they're up to.'

FIVE

Danny and Jack waited a while, then followed Taylor and the others, taking care to ensure that they were not spotted. They soon realized that they were following the Chisholm Cattle Trail, trampled flat over the years by countless longhorns heading north for Kansas railheads.

'I've got a hunch,' said Danny, 'that the men we're following are heading straight for the crossing point at Red River Station, or somewhere nearby. And the way they're moving, it looks like they're in a hurry.'

After darkness fell, Jack and Danny continued riding along the cattle trail, keeping a close watch for any sign of Taylor and the others. At ten o'clock they passed close by a bedded-down trail herd, then, at midnight they saw, just off the trail, the glow of a camp-fire. Approaching it cautiously, they could see eight figures lying near to the fire and one sitting on guard with his back to a boulder.

They kept watch on the outlaws, who, after only

four hours, were on the move again, still heading north in the dark, along the Chisholm Trail. Danny and Jack followed them till daylight, then continued to stalk then. They passed another trail herd, this time on the move, and an hour after darkness had fallen they saw the glow of a camp-fire ahead and to one side of the trail. They guessed that the men they were following had set up camp there for the night.

They dismounted and tied their horses inside a small copse well back from the trail. Then they advanced cautiously on foot. The fire was burning on a stretch of ground studded with small rocky outcrops, and adjacent to a small group of trees.

As Danny and Jack drew closer, taking cover behind the outcrops, they could see that nine men, all seated on the ground, were in camp. The horses were tethered well back from the far side of the fire. Taylor and another man were seated apart from the others, with their backs near to the trees. They appeared to be in close conversation.

'Wish we could hear what they're saying,' Danny whispered to Jack. 'Let's slip into those trees and sneak up closer to them. Maybe we can get some idea of what they're up to. We can't be far from the Red River now.'

Fifteen minutes later, after moving with infinite caution, they stood, side by side, behind a bush at the edge of the copse, about twelve feet from Taylor and his companion. Also in view, but further away, were the other seven men in the party.

After a short pause, Taylor and the other man

resumed their conversation, which, in the still night air, was clearly audible to the two brothers. They chatted for a while about some recent operations carried out by Brown and his gang. During this conversation, it became clear to the listeners that Taylor's companion was called Casey Brown, and that he was the leader of a band of outlaws. Then Taylor changed the subject.

'You figured out yet, Casey,' he asked, 'which three men to send to join up with that short-handed trail herd outfit tomorrow?'

'Yes,' replied Brown, 'it'll be Murray, Gilbert and Chapman. They've all done some cowpunching in the past. I'll send them off early in the morning to find Varney's trail herd. I reckon it should be somewhere near Red River Station, a little way west of here. Varney's probably aiming to cross the Red tomorrow.'

'And you reckon we should take the herd over in Indian Territory?' asked Taylor.

'That's what I reckon,' Brown replied. 'The rest of us'll cross the Red River tomorrow and shadow the herd. We'll leave the trail boss Varney in charge until the herd's fifteen miles or so south of the Kansas border, then we'll take it over.

'We'll send up a smoke signal before dark to let our men with the herd know that we'll be moving in on the camp at midnight. Then Murray and the others'll be waiting to help us from the inside. I reckon it'll be easy. Those trail hands won't know what's hit them.'

Danny now had the information he required.

'Let's go,' he whispered to Jack, then paused as Taylor pulled something out of his vest pocket, struck a match, and looked at the object in his hand.

'A mighty handsome timepiece you've got there,' Brown observed. 'You come by it legal?'

'Not hardly,' Taylor replied. 'You remember me telling you how we finished off that ex-Ranger Brannigan. He was wearing this watch when I shot him. It sure does keep good time.'

'Let's go,' whispered Danny once again. He was seething with anger.

As they slowly started to turn, there was the slightest of sounds behind them, and the muzzle of a six-shooter was forcibly jammed into each of their backs.

'Make a move and you're dead,' said a voice behind them.

The brothers froze, and the man behind the guns called out to Brown and Taylor.

'It's Butler here,' he shouted. 'Come and see what I've found.'

The two outlaws ran over and took the weapons off Danny and Jack, who were then led towards the fire. They were closely inspected by Brown and Taylor and their men.

'You know these men?' Taylor asked Brown.

Brown shook his head, then turned to Butler, the man who had left the party to ride into Fort Worth with Delaney. Butler had purchased ammunition and certain other items for the outlaws, and had then headed north to meet up with them near the Red River.

'What were these men doing?' Brown asked.

'Listening to you two talking,' Butler, replied. 'I watched them a while before I jumped them. I wouldn't have known they were around if I hadn't heard a horse snicker as I was riding towards camp.

'I found their mounts hidden in some trees just off the trail. It seemed like somebody might be watching you, and I figured I'd better locate them and get the drop on them if I could.'

'Search them and their saddle-bags for anything showing who they are,' said Brown.

When the search had produced nothing helpful, Brown spoke to Danny.

'What's your name?' he asked curtly.

'Bradley,' Danny replied, 'and this is my brother with me.'

'Well, Bradley,' said Brown, 'if that really is your name, which I doubt, maybe you'd like to tell us why you've been spying on us.'

'It was like this,' said Danny. 'My brother and me, we're out of a job just now, and when we saw you men ahead of us, we figured that whatever your business was, maybe you could do with a couple more hands. But before riding in and asking for work, we figured we'd better sneak up in the dark and look you over. And that's all we were doing.'

'I don't believe a word of what you say,' said Brown, a suspicious man by nature.

He ordered two hands to take the prisoners to a position near the fire, and to bind them hand and foot. As Danny and Jack were led away, Taylor turned to Brown.

'What d'you aim to do with those two?' he asked.

'It's clear,' Brown replied, 'that they must have heard us talking about taking over that trail herd. We've got to get rid of them somehow.'

For a while they discussed possible ways of dealing with their prisoners. Then Brown called over Butler and Murray, both big, strong men, and told them of the plan for the disposal of Danny and Jack.

'The Red's not far away,' he said, 'and the place you want to aim for is the place east of where we crossed last time, where the bank's pretty steep and there's a fair depth of fast-running water.'

Butler and Murray walked over to Jack and Danny, and by the light of the fire they closely examined the ropes around their wrists and legs. They tied their legs more tightly together, then gagged the two prisoners.

Then they brought four horses over, and hoisted Danny up to lie face down over the back of one of the horses. During this manoeuvre, Danny was able, unnoticed, to pluck the knife from the sheath attached to the back of Butler's belt. Holding it between his hands, he concealed it as best he could.

The two men lifted Jack into position over the back of another horse, then they mounted their own and led the prisoners' horses off to the north. Jack and Danny suspected that they were facing death, but they had no idea as to when, where and how Brown intended that they should die.

With infinite care, Danny held the handle of the

knife between his two hands, with the sharp blade resting on the rope holding his wrists together. Then he started sawing on the rope. He was only able to achieve a very small back and forward movement of the blade across the rope, and he realized that it could be some time, even if he managed to retain hold of the knife, before his hands were free.

He sawed away steadily as the four horses moved northwards through the darkness, and was still sawing when they reached the south bank of the Red River twenty minutes later, and turned to ride eastward along the bank. Minutes later, the rope finally parted and Danny clasped his hands tightly together with the knife between them, hoping that in the darkness the fact that his hands were free would pass unnoticed.

When they came to a halt again, the brothers could hear the water running fast below them and they sensed that at the point at which the horses were standing the bank was almost perpendicular.

The two outlaws pulled Danny and Jack off their horses and laid them on the ground at the top of the bank. Then, simultaneously, they pushed the two prisoners over the edge and into the water below.

Unlike the majority of cowboys, who were unable to swim and had an intense fear of deep water, Danny and his bothers had been encouraged by their father, when they were living in Fort Worth, to learn to swim in a nearby lake, and all three were expert swimmers.

But Danny knew, as they were falling towards the water, that handicapped as they were, he had to act quickly if he and Jack were both to stay alive. When he hit the water the knife was already grasped firmly in his hand, ready for use. As the current quickly took them out of the view of Butler and Murray, staring down through the darkness from above, he reached out desperately and caught hold of Jack.

He held his brother's head above water with his left hand and arm, and with the knife in his right hand he started on an attempt to cut the rope holding his brother's hands together. It was a difficult task, particularly in the darkness, and Jack suffered several cuts on the hands and wrists in the process.

They had moved downstream almost a mile before Jack's hands were freed and he was able to keep himself afloat. Staying close together, they pushed towards the south bank, fetching up on a sandbank jutting out into the river from a gently sloping bank.

Exhausted, they removed their gags, then lay in the shallow water on top of the sandbank for a spell before cutting the ropes binding their legs. Then they staggered out of the water, climbed to the top of the bank and lay there for a short time, cold and wet.

'You all right, Jack?' asked Danny.

'I am now,' Jack replied, 'but for a while there I thought we were goners. Where in blazes did you get that knife?'

'Took it off Butler when they were lifting me on to

the horse,' Danny explained. 'It was lucky for us he was carrying it.'

They squeezed as much water out of their clothing as they could, then waited for the dawn. When the sun came up it was in a clear sky, and soon they could feel the warmth of its rays. They basked in the sunshine for a while. Then Jack spoke.

'What do we do now?' he asked.

'We'll head for Red River Station,' Danny replied. 'We'll keep well clear of the place where Brown and the others were camping, though I reckon that by now they'll have left there to cross the Red. And we'd better keep away from any trail herds we might see on the way.

'When we reach Red River Station we'll buy horses, weapons and ammunition, and some provisions.'

He took his jacket off, pushed his fingers through a gap in the lining, and pulled out a thin, oilskin-covered package which he unfolded to reveal a collection of banknotes and the letter which Ranger Captain Ford had given him in Amarillo. The notes and the letter were undamaged.

'A good thing I hid this package away,' said Danny. 'There's enough money here to keep us going for a while. Let's go.'

Walking westward, and some way south of the river, they headed for Red River Station. Half-way there, and looking towards the north-west, they could see in the distance a herd of longhorns being driven across the river.

'That could be Varney's trail herd,' said Danny,

'and likely three of Brown's hands'll have joined the trail crew now.'

When they reached Red River Station they called first at the livery stable, where they bought a couple of saddle horses. They asked the liveryman, a pleasant, cheerful middle-aged man called Dixon, about the trail herd which had just crossed the river. He told them that it was the Box K herd in charge of trail boss Varney.

When he had paid the bill, Danny told Dixon that he had a brother, Jimmy Brannigan, at present in Fort Worth and staying at the Murray Hotel, and he wanted to get a message to him urgently. He asked Dixon the best way to send this message.

'It so happens,' said Dixon, 'we have a telegraph office along the street on the left. The operator there'll send the message for you.'

They thanked the liveryman and walked along to the telegraph office, where Danny wrote down a message for transmission to Jimmy. It read: 'Waiting for you at hotel Red River Station. Follow Chisholm Trail to get here. Danny'.

They headed towards the store back along the street.

'You reckon Jimmy'll get here safely?' asked Jack.

'I'm sure he will,' Danny replied, 'around two days from now. When he gets here, we'll follow Varney's trail herd and think of some way of upsetting the outlaws' plan to steal the cattle.

'We've plenty of time to catch up with the herd before Brown and Taylor make their move. But we've got to keep out of their sight, and we've got to talk with Varney alone, well before the outlaws are due to make their play.'

On reaching the store, they went inside and bought weapons and ammunition, together with the provisions and other items needed for a long spell of camping out along the trail. Then they booked a room at the hotel and settled down to await Jimmy's arrival.

SIX

Jimmy rode into Red River Station two days later and was soon reunited with his brothers. They told him of their capture by the outlaws and of their subsequent escape; also of their plan to thwart Brown and Taylor.

They crossed the Red River early the following morning, and for the next eleven days adjusted their pace so that they were gradually overhauling the Box K trail herd and the outlaws who were shadowing it. They knew that the herd would probably be averaging only eleven miles or so a day.

When they judged that they were about thirty miles behind the herd and about three days away from the outlaws' coming attempt to steal it, they veered to the west, well away from the Chisholm Trail, then rode parallel to it at a fair pace, keeping a close watch for Taylor and Brown and their men.

It was around noon when Jimmy called out and pointed to a rider, moving in the same direction as themselves, who had suddenly appeared at the top of a distant rise ahead. The brothers took cover, and watched the rider through field glasses as he was joined by six others.

'That's Taylor and the others, for sure,' said Danny. 'The trail herd can't be that far away. I reckon we'd better ride on the other side of the trail from now on. There'll be less chance of us being spotted.'

After waiting for a while, they crossed to the far side of the Chisholm Trail, then rode parallel to it, in a northerly direction. They continued at a fast pace, and at about four in the afternoon they caught a distant glimpse of the herd to their left. It was still strung out and moving, but they guessed that before long it would be reaching the selected bed-ground for the night.

They continued riding north for a further hour, then made camp for the night.

'Tomorrow,' said Danny, as they sat eating supper, 'we'll find a place close to the cattle trail where we can lie in wait for Varney the trail boss while he's scouting ahead for grass and water and the next bed-ground.'

Early the following morning, they rode closer to the trail, following it northwards. Looking to the south, they could see no sign of the herd or riders.

'This'll do,' said Danny, as they approached a low ridge running parallel to the trail. 'We'll hide behind this ridge till the trail boss comes along. Let's hope we can catch him alone.'

It was around three in the afternoon when they caught sight of a rider trotting towards them from the north. He looked like Varney. Danny looked to the south and west. He could see no sign of cattle or other riders. He and his brothers rode over the top of the ridge and down towards the trail boss.

He halted as they approached him, his right hand close to the handle of his six-gun. As the brothers stopped in front of him, Varney looked closely at Jack and Danny.

'Ain't I seen you two before?' he asked.

'You have,' Danny replied. 'It was in Fort Worth, when you were looking for trail hands.'

'I remember,' said Varney, suspiciously, 'and I'm a mite curious about what you're doing here in Indian Territory.'

'I'm Danny Brannigan,' said Danny, 'and these are my brothers Jack and Jimmy. We've brought some news for you. And it ain't good.'

From his pocket he took out the letter from Captain Ford, and handed it to the trail boss.

'I'd like you to read this,' he said, 'before we explain the situation here.'

When Varney had finished reading the letter, Danny continued:

'The three men who killed our father,' he said, 'joined up near Fort Worth with another gang led by an outlaw called Casey Brown. They aim to steal your herd before you reach the Kansas border. They're following you now.'

The news was obviously a shock to Varney.

'Just south of the Red,' Danny went on, 'I think you hired three hands called Murray, Gilbert and Chapman. They're all Casey Brown's men, waiting to help him when the time comes to steal the herd. Brown's going to send up a smoke signal to warn those men when he and the others are ready to move in on you.'

He went on to tell Varney of the recent capture by the outlaws of himself and Jack, and of their sighting of the gang on the previous day.

'From what we heard Brown say just before they captured Jack and me,' he said, 'they plan to steal your herd when you're around fifteen miles south of the Kansas border.'

'I did hire the men you mentioned,' said Varney. 'The question is, what do we do now? I ain't lost a herd before, and I don't aim to lose one now.'

'We'll join up with you to help,' said Danny, 'but before we do, you and your men had better take those three new hands prisoner. They saw me and Jack when we were captured.'

'I'm going back to the herd now,' said Varney. 'It'll be reaching the bed-ground in a couple of hours time. We'll capture Murray and the other two while they're asleep, and tie them up good. You three can ride in at dawn. We'll be expecting you. Then we'll figure out how to deal with the rest of the gang.'

Danny and his brothers rode back to the place at which they had awaited Varney's arrival, and camped there for the night.

In the morning, after sun-up, they rode south until they reached the herd, which was being allowed to graze, while gradually drifting north. They rode up to Varney, who was standing near the chuckwagon with his ramrod Jarvis and several of his hands. The trail boss introduced them to Jarvis and the others then pointed to the chuckwagon.

'We've crammed the three outlaws in there,' he

said. 'Didn't have no trouble with them. Caught them all asleep and tied them up. Figured we'd best keep them out of sight in daylight.'

'I reckon you figured right,' said Danny. 'Us three'll take their places, and I doubt if Brown and the others will notice the difference, from a distance. Did you get any idea from Murray and the others what Brown and Taylor were going to do with the herd after they'd stolen it?'

'I asked them,' Varney replied, 'but they just weren't talking. We'll be throwing the cattle on the trail soon. We'll sure be glad of your help.'

'Just say where you want us,' said Danny, 'but before we start work we'd like to talk about how to deal with those seven outlaws out there. They're all used to handling guns, and I reckon they're all willing to kill to get what they want. We have a few ideas about how we might deal with them.'

'Let's hear them,' said Varney. 'We have a few rifles with us and the trail hands have brought their six-guns along. But they're a long way from being gunfighters. It's been on my mind all night about how we should tackle those outlaws when they show up.'

'It seems to me,' said Danny, 'that it's not a good idea for us to carry on not knowing just exactly when and how we're going to be attacked. I reckon we should carry the fight to them. I reckon we should go after the seven outlaws out there before the time comes when they plan to hit us. And that means that we should go tonight.

'They don't know we're on to them, and if we hit

them in the middle of the night, we've a good chance of surprising them and capturing them without a lot of gunplay.'

'Damned if you ain't right,' said Varney. 'I hadn't thought of that. But it means we've got to find out just where they're camping tonight.'

'Probably not far away from the bed-ground,' said Danny, 'and west of the trail. Me and Jimmy'll ride out soon after dark and locate the camp. They've probably got a small fire going. Then we'll come back for you and the others and lead you straight there later in the night.'

'All right,' said Varney. 'We'd better put the herd on the trail now. Two of you can ride flank and the other one drag.'

They reached the next bed-ground without incident, and after supper Danny and Jimmy rode a mile to the west in the darkness, then turned south.

They had ridden in this direction no more than a couple of miles, when, from the crest of a rise, they spotted the dim glow from a camp-fire, ahead and to the right, about six hundred yards distant. They rode on a little further and dismounted behind a patch of brush.

'You go ahead on foot, Jimmy,' said Danny. 'I know you can move around in the dark a lot quieter than me. I'll wait here with the horses. Count how many men there are in the camp, and see if you recognize any of them. You know what Taylor and his two men look like. As for Brown, he's over six feet – taller than all the others – and he's beetle-browed and bearded.'

'Right,' said Jimmy, and melted into the darkness.

He was back forty minutes later, startling Danny, who had seen or heard nothing to warn him of his brother's imminent arrival.

'There are six men in the camp,' said Jimmy, 'all taking supper. And there are six horses. Brown and Chako and Wilson are all there. But there ain't no sign of Taylor.'

'That's mighty odd,' said Danny. 'We know he was with them two days ago. Where in blazes can he be?'

Danny and Jimmy rode back to the herd and told Varney that they had located the outlaws' camp, and that Taylor was missing.

'Maybe he's ridden into Kansas for some reason,' said Varney. 'It ain't all that far away.'

At midnight, Varney rode off with the three brothers, the ramrod and two trail hands, leaving the cook and three trail hands with the herd and the three prisoners, all securely bound. They stopped at the brush patch where Danny had waited earlier.

'I reckon this is a good place to leave the horses,' said Danny, 'but before we all go ahead on foot, I think we should let Jimmy go into the camp alone, to check on the situation.'

'You sure about that?' asked Varney, mindful of Jimmy's youth.

'Did you ever hear of a Texas Ranger called Seth Barnes?' asked Danny.

'It so happens I *have* heard of him,' said Varney. 'He's a distant relative of my mother. He was an Army Scout before he joined the Rangers.'

'That's right,' said Danny. 'Seth was a friend of my father's, and he lived on the ranch with us. He was killed at the same time as my father. But before he died, he spent a lot of time teaching Jimmy the skills of tracking and stalking. And he reckoned that he'd never had a better pupil. I don't think there's anybody here better qualified than Jimmy to check on the situation in the camp there before we move in.'

'I'm sorry to hear about Seth,' said Varney, 'and I reckon you're right about your brother.'

Moments later, Jimmy faded into the darkness. When he reappeared thirty minutes later, he told them that there were still only six men in the camp. Five were sleeping around the fire, and the sixth, who appeared to be on guard, was seated on a small boulder in the shadows, well back from the fire. 'Occasionally,' said Jimmy, 'his head was nodding.'

For a short while, they discussed the plan of attack. Then, in silence, they all moved closer to the camp, and stopped out of sight of the guard, whose location had been pointed out by Jimmy.

Danny and Varney moved silently forward, leaving the others behind, and came up close behind the guard. They could see the five sleeping men around the fire, and they noted that the guard's chin appeared to be resting on his chest. The trail boss dropped a noose over the guard's head and immediately tightened it around his neck, so that his shout of warning to the sleeping men was strangled at birth.

Holding the noose tight, Varney, with Danny's help, disarmed the guard, dragged him backwards, gagged him, and bound him so that he was unable to move. Then the intruders moved silently in on the five sleeping men, each of whom was rudely awakened at the same instant, to face a cocked pistol. They were then disarmed, securely bound, and laid on the ground close to the fire.

As Danny and the others stood looking down at the outlaws, Brown started as he recognized Jack and Danny, standing close to him. He stared up at them.

'No, we didn't drown in the river, Brown,' said Danny, 'and we're looking forward to handing you and the others over to the law. But we're wondering where your friend Taylor is. Me and my brothers particularly wanted to see him. Maybe you'd tell us where he's gone.'

'Go to hell!' said Brown, fury at his capture showing in his eyes.

Danny and his brothers walked a few paces to stand over Chako and Wilson, who were lying side by side on the ground.

'It's been a long chase for us, Chako and Wilson,' said Danny, 'since you and Taylor murdered our father Joe Brannigan and his partner Seth Brown on the Lazy B in New Mexico Territory. But now you've reached the end of the road. Soon, you'll be handed over to the law. All we have to do now is find Taylor and do the same with him.'

At the mention of Joe Brannigan, the two men on the ground started, and stared up at the three brothers. Then they averted their gaze.

The six bound men were slung over the backs of their horses, and were taken back to the herd, to join the three prisoners there.

'That's a lot of prisoners,' said Varney, a little out of his depth. 'What do we do with them?'

'I reckon that what we need to do is guard them pretty close,' said Danny, 'and keep them tied up. They're all dangerous men. When we get the herd to Caldwell we can hand them over to the law.'

'Come daylight,' said Jimmy, 'I'll ride back to the outlaws' camp and check for any sign of Taylor leaving there. Maybe I'll be able to find which way he was headed when he left.'

'I figure,' said Danny, 'that maybe Taylor went on ahead to Caldwell to find a buyer for the herd – a buyer who wouldn't ask too many questions about where the herd had come from. When d'you expect to arrive outside Caldwell, Mr Varney?'

'We should make it by dark, day after tomorrow,' Varney replied. 'I reckon you may be right about Taylor.'

'You can understand,' said Danny, 'that me and my brothers are mighty keen to get our hands on Taylor. As soon as the cattle are bedded down outside Caldwell, Jack and me'll ride into town to see if we can find Taylor before the prisoners here are handed over to the law.

'We'd be obliged if you'd agree to hand them over late on the following day. If Taylor sees them coming into town before we catch him, it's near certain he'll take to his heels pretty quick.'

'All right,' said Varney, 'we'll do that. I ain't forgetting that if it hadn't been for you three, it's likely myself and the crew'd be dead.'

When Jimmy rejoined the trail herd three hours

after dawn, he reported that there were signs of one rider leaving the outlaws' camp towards the north. He lost the horse tracks when they joined up with the myriad of hoofprints left by cattle moving north along the Chisholm Trail.

In Caldwell, Taylor was awaiting the arrival of the herd. It had been arranged that he would stay in town until Casey Brown sought him out there; and that during his stay there he would arrange the sale of the herd to a buyer of dubious reputation called Sadler, to whom Brown had sold stolen cattle in the past. This, Taylor had done on the day after his arrival, after locating Sadler in a saloon directly opposite the hotel in which he himself was staying.

SEVEN

When the Box K herd arrived near Caldwell, Danny and Jack waited till it had been taken off the trail, then took a quick meal and headed for the town. It was early evening when they rode in and commenced their search for Taylor. They had decided that first they would inspect gaming-houses, saloons and eating-places in the hope of locating the outlaw.

In his room at the Central Hotel, overlooking the main street, Taylor rose from the bed on which he had been resting for the past hour. To relieve the tedium of waiting for Brown, he had decided to walk along to the big gambling-house just along the street in the hope of being able to join a game of poker.

Before leaving his room, he walked up to the window and looked down into the street below. As he watched, two riders rode up to the saloon opposite. They dismounted, tied their horses to the hitching-rail, then stepped on to the boardwalk and stood there talking, in the light from the two big lamps hanging outside the saloon.

Taylor turned away from the window and started walking towards the door of the room. Then he stopped abruptly as he realized that there was something familiar about the two men on the boardwalk. He turned, and went back to the window.

As he looked down again at the two men below, they both turned to face one of the lamps, and he could see their faces more clearly. They appeared to bear a strong resemblance to the two young men, calling themselves Bradley, who had been caught spying on himself and Brown near the Red River, and who had supposedly been drowned by Butler and Murray.

Down below, Danny and Jack walked into the saloon, while up in his hotel room the shaken Taylor puzzled over the possible import of what he had just seen. He decided to go down and get a closer look at the two, without being seen by them.

He left the hotel, crossed the almost deserted street and stood outside one of the windows of the saloon. Peeking inside, he had a close view of the two brothers standing near the bar. They were looking around the saloon. Taylor was sure now that they were the two men who had been dropped into the Red.

He went back to his room and sat on the bed, considering the situation. He was wondering just how the two brothers had managed to stay alive, and what they were doing in Caldwell. He was sure that, before they had been captured, they had heard him and Brown discussing the plan to steal the Box K herd.

He decided that he must try to contact Brown and the others right away, to see if the operation had gone according to plan, and if it had, to warn them of the presence of the two brothers in town. By now, they should have taken the herd over and should be fairly close to Caldwell.

Hastily, he collected his things, paid his bill, and left the hotel. Keeping an eye out for the brothers, he walked in the shadows to the livery stable along the street, and a few minutes later he was riding, unobserved, out of town towards the Chisholm Trail.

Not far south of town he spotted a camp-fire in the distance. He rode closer, then dismounted and tethered his horse. Cautiously, he circled the fire at a distance. Soon, he came upon the herd, now bedded down and being circled by two night guards. It was too dark for him to determine whether the two men were from the combined Taylor – Brown gang.

Pausing frequently, he headed towards the fire, and eventually reached a position behind a boulder, from which he could observe the group of men around the fire without being seen. He recognized none of the men who were sitting between him and the fire, talking to one another.

He looked at the nine men seated on the far side of the fire. There was something unnatural about their posture, and straining his eyes, he suddenly realized that he was looking at Brown and the rest of the outlaws, all with hands and feet bound.

Badly shaken, he stared at them, realizing that there was nothing he could do to help them. His thoughts turned to self-preservation and he decided that he must leave the area as quickly as possible. He retraced his steps back to his horse and headed for Indian Territory.

Back in Caldwell Jack and Danny, failing to spot Taylor, had started asking if anyone had seen him, and late in the evening they spoke to a man who thought he'd seen him at the Central Hotel. He remembered the scar an Taylor's cheek.

They walked along to the hotel, where they received confirmation that Taylor had been staying there. They were told that he had paid his bill and left three hours previously. Further enquiries revealed that around the same time he had collected his horse from the nearby livery stable and had ridden out of town.

The liveryman described Taylor's horse as being a big chestnut gelding with a long white blaze running down its face. The brothers noted that Taylor was no longer riding the palomino on which he had been spotted soon after the murder of their father.

Not knowing that Taylor had spotted them in town, but suspecting that he might have, they wondered if he had ridden back to the herd. They decided to ride back themselves, to join Varney and the others.

When they reached the camp, Varney told them that they had seen no sign of Taylor, although the outlaw might have been spying on them without their knowledge.

'I have a strong feeling,' said Danny, 'that Taylor knows the game's up, and that he's hightailed it for a hiding-place somewhere well away from here. When we've handed the prisoners over in Caldwell tomorrow, me and my brothers'll try to get on his trail again.'

The following morning, Danny and his brothers escorted the nine prisoners to the sheriff's office in Caldwell, while Varney and his ramrod went in search of a buyer for the herd.

Sheriff Turner had just stepped out of his office when he saw the cavalcade of nine bound riders, led by a youthful trio of horsemen, approaching him. Bemused by the spectacle, he stood on the boardwalk as it came to a halt in front of him.

The sheriff looked the prisoners over and started as he recognized three of them, long wanted in Kansas for robbery and murder. He spoke to Danny.

'I see Brown and Butler and Murray there,' he said. 'They're all badly wanted by the law. But what about the rest?'

'They were all planning to steal a herd of longhorns that's waiting just south of here,' Danny replied. 'But we managed to outfox them. If you wouldn't mind slapping them in jail, we'll tell you all about it.'

'We've just about got room for them,' said Turner, and called out a deputy to help him escort the prisoners to the cells at the rear of the building. Then, seated at his desk, he read Captain Ford's letter and listened as the brothers described the events follow-ing the murder of their father.

'That's quite a story,' he said when they had finished. 'So now you reckon to go after this man Taylor?'

'That's right,' Danny replied. 'We ain't got no notion just now where he'll be, but maybe one of his men in the cells, either Chako or Wilson, will give us some idea about where he might have gone.

'Wilson's probably our best bet. Jimmy here looked at the sign at our ranch just after our father and his partner Seth Barnes were killed, and it was clear that Taylor and Chako were the two killers. Wilson was there, but he didn't go into the build-ings where the two killings took place.

'Maybe, if he knows that we believe that he didn't fire either of the shots that killed our father and his partner, he'll figure that if he helps us to find Taylor, the judge'll take it all into account when he passes sentence on him.'

'Maybe you're right,' said Turner. 'It's worth a try. Later on today we'll take him away from the others and put the proposition to him. I'd like you to be there when that happens. Come back here around two o'clock this afternoon.'

'When's the trial likely to be?' asked Jack.

'Two or three days from today,' the sheriff replied.

As he finished speaking, Varney and his ramrod came in. Danny introduced them to the sheriff and they corroborated his account of the thwarted attempt to steal the herd. Varney said he had found a buyer, and the herd would be handed over the following day.

The brothers left to take a meal at a nearby restaurant and returned to the sheriff's office at two o'clock. As they entered, a deputy was leading Casey Brown back to the cells.

'I've been trying to talk with Brown,' said the sheriff, 'but he just ain't saying nothing. Let's get Wilson in and see if we have any better luck with him.'

A few minutes later, a deputy brought Wilson in, to stand in front of the sheriff's desk.

'The Brannigans here,' said Turner, pointing to the three brothers standing at the side of his desk, 'tell me that Chako, with you and Taylor, murdered their father on his ranch in New Mexico Territory, on account of him killing Taylor's son in the course of his duty as a Texas Ranger.

'And on top of that, you joined up with Casey Brown and his gang in a plan to steal a trail herd in Indian Territory. You'll be coming up before Judge Newton in a few days' time, and I'd say here's a fair chance you'll end up hanging at the end of a rope.'

He stopped, and nodded to Danny, why spoke to Wilson.

'My brother Jimmy here,' he said, 'had a good look at the sign you three left behind you on the Lazy B, and we know that while you waited outside, Taylor killed our father, and Chako killed Seth Barnes.

'What me and my brothers want to know is where we're likely to find Taylor now. If you help us on this, the sheriff'll let the judge know, and maybe he'll take it into account when he passes sentence. I say "maybe" because we can't promise anything. It's up to the judge.'

Wilson came to a quick decision.

'You were right,' he said, 'about your father and Barnes. I was there, but I had no hand in the shootings. I've an idea where Taylor might have gone. When we were at his parents' homestead near Trask in Texas, I overheard him telling his father that if the law got too close to him at any time he'd go to a hideout in Texas that he'd been told about. It was northeast of Fort Worth and near the Red River.

'Taylor had never told me and Chako about this place, and I ain't got no idea exactly where it is. What I've just told you is all I know about it.'

Further questioning of Wilson produced no further information of use to the brothers, and the prisoner was led back to the cells.

'I figure he was telling you the truth,' said the sheriff, 'and Taylor might just be scared enough to go to that hideout Wilson was talking about. But how're you going to find it?'

'That's the big question,' Danny replied. 'It's the only lead we have, so I reckon we've got to follow it. If we ride back to Red River Station, we'll be roughly north of Fort Worth. Then we'll follow the Red River eastward, hoping that we come across some sign of Taylor on the way.'

'I guess it's a long shot,' said Turner. 'I'm wishing you the best of luck. You'll be leaving right after the trial?'

'That's right,' said Danny.

When the trial took place two days later, the judge sentenced Chako to death by hanging, also Brown and four of his gang who were known to be involved in murder. Wilson and the rest were given long custodial sentences.

EIGHT

Before the brothers left Caldwell the morning after the trial, Danny sent a telegraph message to Grant Parker, owner of the Circle Dot ranch, whose hands were running the Lazy B while the brothers were away. The message told Grant that two of the killers had been caught and that the brothers were following the third into East Texas.

Four days after leaving Caldwell, they crossed the river and rode into Red River Station, where they intended to start their search for Taylor.

All enquiries about the recent presence of Taylor in Red River Station itself proved fruitless, and on the following morning the brothers headed eastward, confining their search to a band of terrain running adjacent to the south bank of the river.

Two days later, around noon, and with still no news of any sightings of Taylor, they were riding along a flat stretch of ground, with the river some distance away on their left. Jimmy was the first to see, on the trail ahead, a small distant figure running towards them.

As Jimmy pointed it out to his brothers, the figure stumbled and fell, then continued in their direction. They quickened their pace, and as they drew close they could see that it was a sturdy, freckle-faced young boy, no more than ten years old, who was approaching them.

The boy stopped running as he came up to them, and stood, gasping for breath, staring up at the three riders. There was a look of desperation on his face, and he was close to tears. Danny dismounted and walked up to him.

'You in trouble, boy?' he asked.

The boy nodded, but it was a little while before they were able to get from him a clear account of the situation which had sent him out alone, on foot, along the trail.

It appeared that his name was Joey Grant, whose father and mother, Ed and Martha Grant, were running a farm about five miles east. Earlier that day, just after breakfast, Joey had been doing a chore in the barn loft, when he heard some sounds outside.

Looking out through a chink in the timber wall of the barn, he had seen that three riders had stopped outside the door of the nearby house, and had dismounted. One of them was holding his left arm as though it was injured. Joey saw his mother and father come out of the house.

Two of the men drew their guns, and one of them spoke to his father who, when he replied angrily, was struck hard on the side of his head with the man's pistol. Then they all went inside the house, with Joey's father, stunned by the blow, being dragged inside by two of the men.

As Joey, frightened by what he had seem, continued to look towards the house from inside the barn,
the man who had struck his father came out, and
walked towards the door of the barn. Joey quickly
tiptoed to a corner of the loft, and buried himself in
the pile of hay which was standing on the floor.

He had poked a small hole through the side of the
pile, through which he watched, with one eye, the
top of the ladder leading up to the loft. A few
minutes later he had seen the man's head and shoulders appear at the top of the ladder. He did his best
to stay motionless.

Standing on the ladder, the man looked around,
then, apparently satisfied, he disappeared from view.
Moments later, the boy heard the barn door close.

Joey had stayed on in the barn for a while, wondering what he could do to help his parents. He decided
to run for help to their nearest neighbour, Tom
Parkin, whose farm was six miles to the west. Danny
guessed that this was the farm they had just passed.
They had called in to enquire about Taylor, but had
found no one at home.

'You take us back to your farm, Joey,' said Danny,
'and we'll do our best to help your folks. But first,
take us to a spot where we can take a look at the
house without being spotted through the windows by
anybody inside.'

'There ain't no windows in the back of the house,'
said Joey, 'and there's a rise at the back, close to the
house, which we could hide behind.'

'Right,' said Danny. 'You ride with Jimmy here,

and show us the way.'

When they reached the farm, located on the south bank of the Red River, they dismounted at the foot of the rise and climbed to the top. Lying on the ground, they could see the rear wall of the single-storey house directly in front of them, about two hundred yards distant. Just in sight, tied to a hitching rail beyond a front corner of the house, were three horses which, Joey told them, belonged to the three men who had gone inside the house with his parents.

Danny asked Joey to describe the inside of the house, in particular the locations of the rooms, doors and windows. When the boy had finished, Jack asked him a question.

'That little storeroom at the back,' he asked, 'with the window in the side wall. Could me and my brothers get into that room through the window? Is it big enough? And is it likely to be open?'

'Only two of you could make it, I reckon,' Joey replied. 'You and him.' He pointed to Jimmy. 'And it'll be part open, like it always is during the day in fine weather.'

'I see what you're getting at, Jack,' said Danny, and the three brothers considered a plan of action. During the discussion they had to decide, reluctantly, that Joey would have to play a small part. They explained to the boy what they wanted him to do, and he immediately agreed.

While they had been watching the house, there had been no signs of activity outside it, and they decided to make their move. All four of them topped the rise, sprinted over to the rear wall of the house, and stood against it.

They waited a few moments, then Jack poked his head round the corner of the house to take a quick look at the storeroom window.

'You were right, Joey,' he said. 'The window's open, and I reckon me and Jimmy can get through that window, but not Danny!

The three brothers moved silently round to the window. Danny loosened the catch which was holding it half-open, and slowly opened it wide. He could see that the door to the living-quarters was closed. He helped first Jack, than Jimmy, to climb through the window into the room.

As they stood in the confined space, guns in hand, the two brothers could hear the sound of voices on the other side of the door.

Danny and Joey moved further along the side wall of the building, ducking under the one remaining side window. Danny, with Joey close behind him, stopped just short of the corner at the front of the house. Round the corner, and close to it, was the door leading into the building. Further along the wall was a window.

Danny patted Joey on the shoulder, and the boy looked up at him.

'Go now, Joey,' Danny whispered, 'and remember what I told you.'

The boy nodded, walked round to the door, and knocked on it hard. Then he moved sideways, to stand outside the window.

Inside the house, in the living-room, the three men who had forced their way in earlier, were seated at a table, taking a meal. They were the three members of the Barclay gang of outlaws. Barclay, the leader, the one who had pistol-whipped Joey's father, was a big, bearded man, with a pockmarked face and a surly expression. His companions, Gregory and Paxton, were shorter than their leader, but equally villainous in appearance. Gregory was wearing a bandage on the lower part of his left arm.

Martha Grant was working in the kitchen area, and her husband Ed was sitting on a chair, with a bloodstained bandage around his head, still suffering from the effects of the savage blow he had received.

When Joey knocked on the door, Barclay rose and walked quickly over to the window. His two companions stopped eating. Barclay saw Joey standing outside, apparently alone.

'It's only a young boy,' he said. 'Now where could he have come from?'

Martha Grant started, and looked at her husband as Barclay opened the door. His two companions stood up at the table, watching him. Barclay poked his head through the door, looked to left and right, then stepped outside. He turned to face Joey, and took two steps towards him. Silently, Danny slipped around the corner of the house, came up behind Barclay and struck him hard across the head with the barrel of his Peacemaker.

As the outlaw collapsed on the ground, Danny fired a shot into the air, and Joey scampered around to the back of the house. Hearing Danny's signal, Jack and Jimmy ran out of the storeroom and came up behind Gregory and Paxton, who had started moving towards the doorway through which they had seen Danny running towards Barclay.

Before the two outlaws were aware of the danger, each of them felt the muzzle of a six-gun jammed into his back, and heard the shouted command to halt. Both men obeyed, and a moment later they were relieved of their weapons, and were made to sit on the floor with their backs to the wall. Cursing, they stared up into the faces of their youthful captors.

Danny came in, carrying Barclay's revolver. He looked with satisfaction at the two men sitting an the floor.

'The other one's out there,' he said. 'He ain't in no shape to cause us trouble just now.'

Martha Grant ran up to him.

'Joey?' she asked

'He's all right,' Danny replied. 'He's waiting at the back of the house. He sure did a good job helping us to get the better of these three villains.'

She ran out, and reappeared a few minutes later with the boy. Danny introduced himself and his brothers to the Grants.

'I reckon,' he said, 'that we should put these three in the barn till we can get the law to come and pick them up. Is that all right with you, Mr Grant?'

'A good idea,' said the farmer. 'We sure don't want them in here. There's plenty of rope in the barn for tying them up.'

Danny dragged Barclay into the barn while his brothers escorted the other two into the building.

Barclay was now showing signs of coming to. All three men were securely bound hand and foot, and were left lying on the floor. Leaving Jimmy to guard them, Jack and Danny rejoined the Grants in the house.

'Those men in the barn,' said Danny, 'they look like outlaws to me. Was that a bullet wound one of them had in the arm?'

'It was,' Martha Grant replied. 'They made me tend to it.'

'We need to get hold of the Rangers to come and pick them up,' said Danny. 'What's the quickest way of getting in touch with them?'

'There's a small town called Delado, about twelve miles south of here,' said Grant, 'and there's a Ranger called Harper who calls in there regular. He was due there today, and he usually stays one night. I'll ride over there and tell him what's happened here.'

He started to rise from his chair, then slumped down again as a dizzy attack took hold of him. His wife ran to his side.

'You're not going anywhere,' said Danny. 'You rest that head. I'll go myself, right now.'

He turned to Jack.

'Those men in the barn, Jack,' he said, 'they all look like killers to me. We've got to watch them day and night. You spell Jimmy off for a while, and I'll take a turn when I get back.'

When Danny arrived in Delado, it did not take him long to locate Ranger Lon Harper, seated in the small restaurant next to the hotel. He was just finishing a meal. Danny introduced himself, and Harper asked him to sit down.

Danny showed him the letter from Ranger Captain Ford. Then he really grabbed Harper's attention when he told him of the capture of the three men at the Grant farm. At Harper's request, Danny described the three men as accurately as he could. As he did so, Harper's interest mounted.

'I'm pretty certain,' he said, when Danny had finished, 'that you're talking about the Barclay gang. A few days ago, they robbed a bank in Danton, a hundred and fifty miles west of here. They killed a cashier, and one of them was shot in the arm by a townsman as they rode off. It was a while before a posse was organized, and they weren't able to catch up with the gang.

'We've been after this gang for a long time, and they're going to be mighty pleased at headquarters when they hear about this. There's a telegraph office in town. I'm going to send headquarters a message right away to ask them for help in getting the gang back to Fort Worth. Then I'll ride back to the farm with you.'

When they reached the farm, night was falling. A lamp had been lit in the barn, and Harper took a look at the prisoners.

'There's no doubt about it,' he said, 'that's the Barclay gang. I'll stay with you till help gets here. I reckon that'll be day after tomorrow.'

After they had returned to the house, Danny told the Grants and Harper of their suspicion that Taylor might be hiding out somewhere between the farm and the Arkansas border. He gave them a description of Taylor.

'Can't say I've seen him around these parts,' said Harper.

'Maybe I can help,' said Grant. 'Four days ago, I was working in one of the fields close to the river when I saw a rider crossing from the far side. Generally, the Red's low enough to be forded here.

'I walked up to the bank to give him the time of day, but it was clear he weren't in any mood for talk. He just grunted, and rode off to the east, along the riverbank. The thing is, he was a big man, with a scarred left cheek. The scar ran along here.'

He demonstrated with his finger on his own cheek.

'And he was riding a big chestnut, with a white stripe down its face.'

'That's definitely Taylor,' said Danny. 'Now we know that we guessed right about which way he was heading.'

'If Mr Grant would show me in the morning just where Taylor rode out of the river,' said Jimmy, 'I'll take a look at the sign there. Maybe I'll see something useful.'

'I'll take you down there at daylight,' said Grant. 'After what you three've done for us, I'm sure glad I've been able to give you the information about seeing the man you're after.

'If it hadn't been for the Barclay gang turning up here, the three of us would have been visiting friends in Delado at the time you three were passing by the farm.'

Harper and the brothers took turns at guarding

the prisoners overnight, and in the morning Jimmy went to the riverbank with Grant. At just one spot on the bank, where there was a bare patch of ground, he found and memorized a clear set of hoofprints left by Taylor's horse. It indicated that the design of one of the four shoes was slightly different from that of the other three.

The brothers helped to guard the prisoners until the following morning, when two Rangers arrived to escort them to Fort Worth. Then they took their leave of the Grants and the Rangers, and headed east.

NINE

When they camped at the end of the day, the brothers were still without any further information about Taylor's whereabouts. They had not been able to pick up his trail, and they suspected that he was making a point of avoiding contact with people along the way.

The following day went the same way until just after noon, when, from the top of a ridge along which they were riding, they saw, some distance to the south, what appeared to be a large basin of which the bottom was not visible from their position. Just ahead of them the trail forked, the right-hand fork leading towards the basin.

'Wonder if there's anybody living down there,' said Jack.

'Let's take a look,' said Danny. They rode on and took the trail leading to the basin. Jimmy was in the lead, his eyes idly scanning the ground. Suddenly, only about eight yards from the fork, he yelled out and raised his arm, then stopped and dismounted. The others halted.

Jimmy bent down over a patch of bare ground

right on the edge of the trail, and examined it closely. Excited, he turned to his brothers.

'There's a good set of hoofprints here,' he said, 'and they belong to Taylor's horse. Looks like he was heading for that basin.'

'You sure, Jimmy?' asked Danny.

'These prints are the same as the ones I saw at the Grants' farm,' said Jimmy. 'I'm sure of it.'

'Do we ride down and have a look inside that basin?' asked Jack.

'Not just yet,' Danny replied. 'We'll take the left fork there, then ride down the left-hand side of the ridge, out of sight of the basin. We'll leave the horses, climb to the top of the ridge, and watch the basin through our field glasses for a while.'

Twenty minutes later, they were lying on top of the ridge, looking down at the basin. Through the glasses, Danny could see that the trail leading towards it appeared to pass right into it.

Inside the basin, he could see the top of a tall windmill, probably built specially high in order to catch the wind above the basin's rim. It would supply water for whatever operation was being conducted inside the basin. He noticed that near the top of the windmill there was a circular enclosed platform, probably to help in routine maintenance and repair operations.

For a time Danny kept the glasses trained on the point where the trail reached the rim of the basin. Just as he was about to hand the glasses to Jack, a man stepped out from behind a large boulder at the side of the trail and stood looking in their direction.

After a few minutes, he moved out of sight again, and Danny, looking through the glasses at the ground around the top of the basin, saw a rider come into view. He appeared to be slowly circling the rim of the basin. Jimmy and Jack both took turns at looking down at the basin through the glasses, then they all discussed the situation.

'I've got a srong feeling,' said Danny, 'that Taylor's down there. But we can't bring the law in till we're sure.'

'I reckon,' said Jack, 'that we'd better find out more about the folks in that basin before we try to see whether Taylor's there. Somebody around here must know who's in there, and what they're doing.'

'You're right, Jack,' said Danny. 'Let's go to that town Langtry, that the last farmer we spoke with mentioned. I reckon it's only a few miles west of here along the trail. We'll see what's known there about that basin down below.'

When they arrived in Langtry, they decided to spend the night there, and rode their horses up to the livery stable. They found the owner, Wilkin, inside. He was a pleasant-faced, middle-aged man who greeted them with a smile. They asked him if he would care for their mounts.

'Sure,' he said. 'You staying long in town?'

'Likely just one night,' Danny replied. 'We were wondering if you could tell us anything about an outfit that's operating in a big basin five miles west of here. We could see people moving around, but we weren't close enough to take a look inside.'

'The Box D ranch is in the basin you're talking

about,' said Wilkin, 'and maybe it's just as well you didn't go any closer. Anybody trespassing there is liable to get shot at.' He went on to tell them that a stranger from Arkansas, called Devlin, had crossed into Texas five years earlier, and had bought the land in the basin for the stated purpose of establishing a ranch on which he intended to go into the business of horse breeding.

The labour required to construct the ranch buildings, windmill, corral and fences was imported from Arkansas and returned there when the job was completed. Ranch hands, also from Arkansas, then drove in a horse herd. Supplies of all kinds were freighted in regularly from Arkansas.

'What it amounts to,' said Wilkin, 'is that nobody around here really knows what's going on in the basin. Like I said, it's too dangerous for anybody to go snooping around. Devlin reckons he's had to mount guards in the basin, on account of trouble with horse-thieves.

'There's only one man from town who's been in the basin, and that's Doc Haley. He went there once when Devlin was took sick. He said he saw a fair-sized horse-herd there, and a crop of hay. But what took his eye most were two other things.

'The first was the size of the ranch house – twice as big as might have been expected. The second was the circle of twenty big, well-built log cabins which surrounded the house.

'Devlin told Haley that the cabins were for the ranch hands and occasional family visitors. He said that he thought his employees deserved better than the cramped, uncomfortable conditions found in the usual bunkhouse.'

'If that's true, this man Devlin sounds like a good employer,' said Danny. 'Have you ever seen him yourself?'

'He came into town just once,' Wilkin replied. 'He's in his fifties, I'd say, sandy-haired, with a goatee beard. He's slim, average height, and pretty well dressed. He acted pleasant enough when he was in town.

'His foreman, a man called Pascoe, was with him. He was carrying a six-gun, and looked like he knowed how to use it. He's a tall, slim man, mean-looking and clean-shaven.'

'I can see,' said Danny, 'why anybody might be curious about Devlin's operation. It's easy to get the idea that he's got something to hide.'

'That's right,' said Wilkin. ' But there ain't nothing we can do about it.'

After spending the night in Langtry, the brothers returned, without coming in view of the basin, to the point from which they had observed it through the glasses the previous day.

They settled down to watch the basin, and observed that one man, relieved from time to time, was stationed by the trail where it led into the basin. A second man, on horseback, regularly made a slow circuit of the basin, close to its rim. He, too, was relieved at regular intervals.

Just as darkness was about to fall, the two guards rode down into the basin and disappeared from view.

'We'll wait till they're settled down for the night,'

said Danny, 'then we'll go down and look the place over as best we can. We need to find out whether Taylor is there.'

They waited until midnight, then rode to a point on the rim of the basin well away from the point at which the trail led into it. They rode down the slope into the basin, and stopped when they saw distant buildings, outlined against the night sky. The tall windmill was also visible.

'This is where *you* come in, Jimmy,' said Danny, 'because none of us here can do the job better than you. I reckon there's bound to be guards around somewhere. We'll wait here while you scout around and find out just where they are.'

'Right,' said Jimmy, and melted quickly into the darkness. He was away for forty minutes, and startled his brothers by suddenly appearing at their side as they stared towards the buildings.

'I saw those cabins the liveryman talked about,' said Jimmy. 'The other buildings and the cabins are all circled by a wire fence about six feet high, with wires about nine inches apart. There are three gates spaced around this fence, with a guard on each gate.'

'Is the windmill inside the fence?' asked Danny.

'No,' Jimmy replied, 'it's well outside. I took a look at it. It's a four-legged windmill, with a big water-tank at the bottom.'

'I've got an idea, then,' said Danny, 'but first, let's go and have a look at that windmill. Better leave the horses here.'

Jimmy led them to the windmill, and for a few moments Danny stood looking upwards along the ladder towards the vanes. Then he told his brothers what he proposed to do.

'I'll take some of that food and water we've brought with us,' he said, 'and the field glasses, and I'll climb to the top of the windmill. I think there's a closed-in platform up there where I can hide. If there isn't I'll come right down again. Wait for five minutes, and if I don't come down you can leave.

'If I stay, then as soon as it's daylight, I'll watch out for Taylor. If he's there, then there must be a good chance that I'll see him sometime during the day. You two go back to the ridge.

'Take my horse with you, and twenty-two hours from now bring it back to the place where the horses are now. I'll meet up with you there. If I don't turn up, you'll know that something's gone wrong.'

'What if there's trouble with the windmill, and somebody happens to climb up the tower tomorrow?' asked Jack.

'That's a chance I'll have to take,' Danny replied. 'I know the bearings and gears have to be greased now and again, but not all that often.'

He climbed the ladder to the top of the tall tower, to find that the maintenance platform was just sufficiently enclosed to allow him to remain concealed from anyone below. He settled down for the rest of the night, while below, his brothers walked to the horses and rode out of the basin, leading Danny's mount.

When dawn broke, Danny found that he had a good, uninterrupted view of the whole area within the wire fence. The first movement he observed was when a small man wearing an apron came out of an annexe to the big house. From the roof of this annexe projected a smoking chimney. Probably the cook and his cookshack, thought Danny.

The man entered another building attached to the house, and emerged shortly after, to be followed to the cookshack by twelve men, obviously ranch hands. They remained there for a little over half an hour, then came out and dispersed to carry out various chores around the ranch. Danny saw two men ride off to commence their daytime guard duties, and two hands headed towards the horse-herd.

About an hour later, the cook came out again and called to a hand, who walked up to nineteen of the twenty cabins in turn, and knocked on the door. Soon after this, men started to leave their cabins, then walk over to the house, and disappear inside. It was clear from their dress and appearance that they were not ranch hands.

Danny trained his glasses on the men as, one by one, they approached the house. But it was not until he looked at the next but last one to enter that he knew they had caught up with their quarry at last. The man was Taylor, without any doubt.

Taylor came out of the house with another man over an hour later. They walked over to a building not far from the house and came out shortly after with two saddled horses. They mounted and set off. Danny watched them closely, fearing that Taylor might be about to leave the ranch, but the two riders headed further into the basin, and returned to the stable, ninety minutes later. Then Taylor went to his cabin, while the other men entered the house.

Danny continued to watch from his uncomfortable position. He could see the three gates in the fence at which the night guards were posted. In order to avoid being seen by the hands working at various tasks down below, he had either to sit or kneel on the narrow platform. He was looking forward to the time when nightfall would allow him to descend to the ground.

Half an hour after midday, he saw Taylor and other occupants of the cabins heading once again for the ranch house, presumably for a meal. At 3.30 in the afternoon, Taylor and the others had still not left the house, and Danny guessed that they were indulging in some kind of social activity.

There was no doubt in his mind now that the ranch was a haven – and probably a mighty expensive one – for outlaws on the run.

His mind was working on a plan to capture Taylor, when suddenly his worst fears were realized. He spotted a ranch hand passing through a gate in the fence, carrying a metal container with a handle sticking out of the top.

The man walked up to the windmill, and Danny tensed as the hand started climbing up the ladder. It was clear that his intention was to grease the gears and bearings behind the wheel. Hampered by the container, the man made slow progress. Danny could see no way out of a situation which would easily lead to his capture.

The ranch hand was almost half-way up the ladder when Danny heard voices below. Somebody was speaking to the hand on the ladder. Danny was able to make out the words 'Do it tomorrow' just before the hand started to climb back down to the ground.

Shortly after this, Danny risked a downward look. He saw the hand, and another man who fitted Wilkin's description of the foreman Pascoe. The hand went for a horse and rode towards the middle of the basin. Pascoe joined a man who had just come out of the house, and who fitted Wilkin's description of the ranch owner Devlin. After a brief conversation, both men went into the house.

Somewhat shaken by his narrow escape, Danny resumed his watch. Before nightfall, he saw Taylor visit his cabin briefly, then return to the house. He stayed up the tower until Jack and Jimmy were almost due to arrive, then climbed down to the ground and awaited their coming.

When they showed up, all three headed for the ridge, and on arrival there they discussed the problem of capturing Taylor and removing him from the basin without the knowledge of Devlin.

Danny told the others that Taylor's cabin was the same distance from the positions of the two nearest guards at the fence, and they should, in the dark, be able to squeeze through the fence wires and reach the cabin unseen. After capturing Taylor, they could take him out by the same route as the one by which they had entered. They could sling him over Jimmy's horse, and Jimmy could ride with Jack.

The following day they stayed on the ridge, and spent some time discussing details of their plan to capture Taylor. At midnight they left for the basin and rode to the same place, within the basin, where they had left their mounts on their previous visit. Danny handed to Jimmy, for safe-keeping, the roll of banknotes he was carrying, and the letter from Captain Ford.

Carrying some rope with them, they proceeded on foot to a point on the fence midway between two guards. The sky was overcast and they were sure that they were not visible from the points at which the guards were posted.

Jimmy pulled two of the wires further apart to see if he could make enough space for his brothers to pass through without being impeded. The space was ample, and he was surprised at how smoothly the wires moved in the holes which had been drilled through the stout wooden posts.

They decided to negotiate the fence by passing between the wires. To climb over the top strand was likely to cause more noise and disturbance.

The plan was that when Jack and Danny reached the other side of the fence they would go to Taylor's cabin and disable him, then carry him back to the fence. Jimmy would wait a little way back from the fence, and when he heard them return, he would move up to it and help to pass Taylor through. Then they would leave the basin.

Slowly, Jimmy pulled two of the wires further apart, and held them in that position while first Jack, then Danny, passed through. Then Jimmy threw the rope over the fence, and Jack picked it up. He and Danny then started walking toward Taylor's cabin. Jimmy retreated from the fence for a short distance, then stood looking towards it as his brothers disappeared from view.

Jack and Danny walked slowly forward in the direction of the cabin, then suddenly came to a halt as the figures of six men, standing in a row, loomed up in front of them.

TEN

When the brothers had arrived at the fence, the guard at one of the two gates nearest to them had heard a slight scraping noise as Jimmy pulled on the wires. To provide a crude alarm system, each wire had been connected to a gatepost by a coiled spring which held it taut, and the wires had been lubricated where they passed through the posts along the fence.

Each spring passed through a metal sleeve, fixed at one end, and as the spring stretched inside the sleeve, it made the scraping noise which told the guard that a wire on the fence was being disturbed.

When Jimmy had first pulled on the wires, the guard immediately ran silently to the bunkhouse and woke five hands, who dressed hurriedly in the darkness and came out quietly with their weapons. They walked towards the middle of the section of fence which had been disturbed. A hand called Kennedy was in charge.

The six men caught sight of the two intruders and came to a halt.

'Hold it there!' shouted Kennedy. 'We're all

armed, and two of us have shotguns. You haven't got a chance in hell of getting away. Just drop your weapons slow and easy-like, or there'll be two loads of buckshot coming your way.'

'Do like he says, Jack,' muttered Danny. 'The man's right. We ain't got a chance against them.'

They dropped their weapons to the ground. The six men walked up to them, checked them for further weapons, relieved them of the rope, then escorted them towards the house, where the foreman Pascoe, as well as Devlin, slept.

Jimmy, hidden by the darkness from the six ranch hands, clearly heard Kennedy's shouted command, followed shortly after by the sound of receding voices. He had matured considerably since they had set out on the trail of Taylor and the others, and he realized that any intervention on his part at that moment would likely do more harm than good.

He walked back to the horses and stood by them, striving to think clearly. A plan took shape in his mind, and after considering it carefully, he decided to go ahead with it.

He left his brothers' horses where they were, for Devlin's men to find, but he took the two rifles from the saddle holsters. Then he rode out of the basin on his own horse to a small, nearby hollow that they had passed on the way there. It was dotted with small patches of brush, and had a little pool of water, surrounded by a grassed area, at its centre. Here he tethered his horse, leaving enough slack on the rope to allow it to graze and drink. He hid his brothers' rifles in a patch of brush.

Then, carrying some food and drink, the field glasses, and a coil of rope, he started on the one-and-a-half-mile walk back to the place on the ranch where he had left his brothers' horses. As he walked, he wondered about the speedy appearance of the armed ranch hands who had captured his brothers.

A guard, he thought, must somehow have been alerted by the passage of Danny and Jack through the fence. He decided to examine the fence, as closely as was possible in the dark, on his return.

When he reached the point where his brothers' horses had been tethered, he found that they had been removed, obviously by Devlin's men. Cautiously, he moved on to the point on the fence where his brothers had passed through.

He felt the wires where they passed through holes in the post. They all fitted loosely in the holes, and appeared to be coated with grease, near to the posts. He felt sure now that any movement of a wire from its normal position somehow sent an alarm signal to a guard at one of the gates.

He walked over to the windmill tower, climbed the ladder to the platform at the top, and settled down there to await the dawn.

When Jack and Danny were taken to the ranch house after their capture, Kennedy first woke Pascoe the foreman, who had them taken into the house, guarded by two of the men. He sent another two men to look for the prisoners' horses, then he woke Devlin.

When the rancher came into the room where the

prisoners were being held, he looked closely at them, then spoke to Pascoe.

'D'you know them?' he asked.

'No,' Pascoe replied, 'and I'm mighty curious about them being found inside the fence with a coil of rope.'

'Search them,' said Devlin. 'See if we can put a name to them.'

The search produced no information as to the prisoners' identities. Devlin spoke to them.

'It riles me considerable,' he said, 'when anybody comes on to the Box D without my permission. Maybe you'd tell me just what you're doing here in the middle of the night.'

When Danny and Jack remained silent, Devlin turned to Pascoe.

'It looks like we're going to have to beat the truth out of them,' he said, 'but before we do that, I want all our guests to take a look at them. Maybe one of them can tell us who they are.

'Put them into that empty cabin, with a guard outside, for the rest of the night, and after breakfast I'll get the guests to look them over.'

Tied hand and foot, in a cabin next to Taylor's, the brothers spent an uncomfortable night. While the guests were having breakfast, the prisoners were untied and taken out, to stand outside the house.

At Devlin's request, the guests came out after breakfast, one by one, and looked at Danny and Jack. Each of them, except Taylor, who was the last one out, shook his head. Taylor looked at them closely, then walked up to the rancher and Pascoe.

He told them that he had seen the two prisoners twice before, but that both men were unknown to him. The first time had been when they were caught spying on himself and Casey Brown when they were camped near Red River Station, planning a forth-coming operation, and that they had somehow escaped death by drowning.

The second time was in Caldwell, where he had seen them in town and had left before they could see and recognize him. He figured they might have had something to do with the capture of Casey Brown.

'Looks like they might have followed you here,' said Devlin. 'I'm not happy about that. Maybe they're lawmen. We've got to get rid of them. But not here.'

He spoke to Pascoe.

'First thing tomorrow,' he said, 'you and a couple of men take these two across the river into Indian Territory and finish them off. Make it look like an accident or a killing by Indians. I'm leaving that up to you. Just so long as their deaths can't be traced back to anybody at the Box D.'

Pascoe nodded, and told the two guards to take the prisoners back to the cabin.

A worried-looking Taylor spoke to Devlin.

'Finding those two on the ranch like that ain't good,' he said. 'I don't reckon I'm safe here. I aim to leave this morning.'

'Please yourself,' said Devlin, 'but don't expect a refund. I'm blaming you for them being here.'

Back in the cabin, the two prisoners discussed the situation. They had heard snatches of Devlin's conversation with Pascoe, and they suspected that on

113

the following day, unless by some miracle they could escape beforehand, they would surely die. They wondered how Jimmy was faring, never dreaming that he was presently watching events from the top of the windmill tower.

'I'm hoping,' said Danny, 'that Taylor and Devlin don't know anything about Jimmy being here with us, and that they ain't out searching for him.'

Jimmy, from his position at the top of the windmill tower, saw the brothers being taken over to the house to be inspected by the guests. He recognized Taylor from descriptions he had been given of him. He saw the prisoners being escorted back to the cabin, and saw Taylor return to his shortly after.

An hour later he saw Taylor leave his cabin and go into the stable. Five minutes later, Taylor rode out on the chestnut and Jimmy followed him with the glasses as he rode out of the basin and turned on to the trail leading to Langtry. Soon he was out of sight.

Jimmy figured that Taylor was quitting the hide-out, scared by the appearance there of Danny and Jack. It seemed that the end of the pursuit of his father's murderer had not yet been reached.

He stayed on the windmill tower for the rest of the day. His brothers were kept in the cabin all day, with a guard outside the only door leading into it. The guard was relieved every four hours. Just as darkness was failing, three additional guards took up their positions at the three fence gates.

At ten in the evening, Jimmy climbed down the tower and, glad of the exercise, he walked out of the basin to collect his horse and the two rifles from the hollow. Returning to the basin, he tethered the horse as before, well outside the fence. He waited by the horse until a quarter to three in the morning, then walked up to the fence. He was aiming to arrive at the cabin holding the prisoners at about three and a half hours before the guard was due to be relieved. The sky was overcast, as on the previous night.

Carrying a length of rope, he walked to a fence post midway between two gates. Taking care not to apply pull on any of the wires, and working slowly and carefully in the dark, he fastened the rope around the top of the post, then formed loops in the free end of the rope at various heights above the ground. He cut off the surplus length of rope and threw it over the fence, ready to take to the cabin.

Holding on to the top of the post, Jimmy climbed upwards placing his feet in the loops until he was able to place one foot on top of the post and jump down to the ground on the far side of the fence.

He removed the makeshift rope-ladder from the post, and refastened it so that it hung down his side of the fence. With his back to the fence, he stood motionless for a while, listening, and preparing himself for the next stage of his rescue attempt.

The problem now was how could a boy, barely sixteen, tackle the guard outside the cabin without raising the alarm? Jimmy, with ambitions to be a lawman in a few years' time, had discussed with his mentor Seth Barnes, ways of overcoming enemy guards in the dark without actually killing them, and without giving them the chance of raising the alarm.

Seth had two favourite methods, both dependent on taking up a position, unnoticed, behind an unsuspecting victim.

'Use a piece of thin, strong rope,' he had told Jimmy. 'Hold it in both hands, slip it over his head, then around his neck, and pull on it hard. If a man's wind's cut off, he ain't in much of a shape to fight back, and he'll soon pass out.

'Mind you, this is most likely to work if the man holding the rope is the stronger of the two. The other way is called "buffaloing" or "pistol-whipping". It's used now and then by some law officers to avoid killing somebody they're trying to arrest. They knock him over the head with the barrel of their pistol. If it's done right, he's stunned for a while, and wakes up in a cell with a sore head.'

Seth had demonstrated both techniques to Jimmy, pointing out the best points of impact for the pistol-whipping method.

Watching out for the guard, Jimmy started walking slowly towards the cabin holding his brothers, and when he came up behind it he stood pressed against the wall. Listening, and bracing himself for the coming encounter, he heard a faint cough from the far side of the cabin. He moved soundlessly round the corner and along the side wall, then peeped around the corner and along the front wall of the cabin. His gun was in his hand.

He could see a dim figure standing motionless, seven feet away, near to the door, and with his back to the wall. Jimmy steeled himself for an encounter, the outcome of which could mean life or death to him and his brothers. He laid the coil of rope gently on the ground.

The guard, a short, slim man, was looking straight ahead. As Jimmy watched him, he felt in his pocket for tobacco and paper, then started to roll a cigarette. With the three guards at the fence acting as the first line of defence, he had little fear of any direct attack on himself.

The guard finished rolling the cigarette and put it in his mouth. Then he struck a match on the wall and turned his head against the slight breeze. As the match flared up, partially blinding the ranch hand, Jimmy made his move. He darted up behind the guard, and struck him a blow on the head with his pistol-barrel, doing his best to copy the Seth Barnes technique.

With only the faint beginnings of a yell of alarm, the guard fell to the ground and lay still. Jimmy turned the key in the door, opened it, and dragged the guard inside. Then he went for the rope, came back, and closed the door behind him. By the light of a small oil-lamp standing on a table, Jimmy saw his brothers lying bound on the floor. They were staring up at him, hardly believing what they were seeing. Danny spoke.

'Jimmy!' he said. 'How in blazes did you manage to get here? On second thoughts, cut us free and tell us later.'

Jimmy cut the ropes binding his brothers. Then they securely trussed and gagged the guard, who was showing signs of coming to. Before they left the cabin Danny took the guard's revolver.

Jimmy led the way to the fence, and they all

climbed over, using the makeshift rope ladder, which they took with them as they ran to Jimmy's horse. Jimmy handed Jack and Danny their rifles.

'So far, so good,' said Danny, 'but now there's a problem of three men, one horse. It just don't add up.'

'Trouble was,' said Jimmy, 'I had to leave your horses where they were after you were caught, so that they'd figure you two were alone. But there ain't no problem. You remember seeing that corral not far from the windmill tower?'

'I remember,' said Danny.

'Well,' said Jimmy, 'your two horses are in there. And the saddles and bridles are lying on the ground just outside the corral fence. I saw them earlier today.'

'I can see, Jimmy' said Danny, 'that you've got a pretty brainy head on top of them shoulders – which is why Jack and me are standing here.'

He turned to Jack.

'Let's go for them horses,' he said. 'Wait here, Jimmy.'

When Jack and Danny returned, they all rode out of the basin, and paused on the rim. There was no sound of pursuit. Jimmy told his brothers that, with luck, it would be three hours or more before the relief guard turned up at the cabin, and their escape was discovered. He also told them that Taylor had left the ranch during the morning of the previous day, and that the outlaw had taken the trail leading towards Langtry.

'Let's get on Taylor's trail before it gets cold,' said

Danny. 'We'll call in at Langtry to send a message to Ranger headquarters about the Box D. I reckon that when Devlin realizes we've got clear away, he'll be bound to close down the operation. But maybe the Rangers'll be in time to catch up with him and some of his guests.'

Two miles west of Langtry, not long after daybreak, Jimmy had a clear sighting of the distinctive hoofprints of Taylor's horse. They rode on into town and headed for the livery stable. Wilkin came out of the stable as they rode up and dismounted.

Danny told him about their pursuit of Taylor, and recent events on the Box D. As the liveryman listened, his eyebrows rose higher and higher.

'Well I'm dinged!' he said, when Danny had finished. 'I always figured there was something fishy about that place.'

'I want to send a message to the Ranger headquarters at Fort Worth about Devlin's operation,' said Danny. 'Can you help me with that?'

'Sure,' said Wilkin. 'There's a westbound stagecoach passes a few miles south of here around noon. Write a message down, and I'll get somebody to ride out and hand it to the driver.'

Danny thanked the liveryman, and went inside the stable to write the message. In it, he told Ranger Captain Bixby at Fort Worth about Devlin's use of the Box D, near Langtry, as a haven for outlaws. He told Bixby that following the escape of himself and his brothers, Devlin and his guests could have decided to leave. He said that Taylor had already left, and that he and his brothers were on the outlaw's trail.

119

When Danny had handed the message to Wilkin, Jack described Taylor, and asked the liveryman if a man fitting Taylor's description had been in town the previous day.

'Not that I knows of,' Wilkin replied. 'If a stranger like that had been in town, I reckon I'd have heard about it.'

Jack had an idea.

'Is there a fording-place on the Red near here?' he asked.

'Yes, there is,' Wilkin replied. 'It's due north of town.'

'It struck me,' said Jack, 'that maybe Taylor's crossed over into Indian Territory. The law ain't so likely to catch up with him over there.'

'You could be right, Jack,' said Danny. 'When we leave here, we'll go to the ford and Jimmy can look for the hoofprints of Taylor's horse.'

He turned to Wilkin.

'If we don't come back here soon,' he said, 'it'll mean that we know Taylor's crossed the river, and that we're following him. Will you tell that to the Rangers when they get here?'

'Sure,' said Wilkin.

They thanked the liveryman, then went over to the store, where they purchased ammunition, one revolver to replace the one taken from Jack at the Box D, and provisions for the days ahead. Then they headed north for the fording-place on the Red River.

When they reached the river, Danny and Jack stayed back while Jimmy studied the ground ahead. It was only a matter of minutes before he called out and waved them on. They rode up to him.

'You were right, Jack,' said Jimmy, pointing to the ground. 'There's a good, clear set of hoofprints there. There ain't no doubt that Taylor's crossed over the river.'

They forded the river, and Jimmy located hoofprints left by Taylor's mount on the far side. They indicated that the outlaw was heading roughly northwest. The brothers struck off in that direction.

ELEVEN

When Taylor left the Box D, he was in a confused state of mind. Three times recently he had encountered Danny and Jack, and the encounters had taken place many miles apart. They could, he thought, hardly be coincidence. And at the time of the second encounter, it was only by chance that he had not been captured and sentenced with Brown and the others.

Even though he knew that the two intruders on the Box D were going to be killed, he could not be sure that they had not already passed information about him and his presence on the ranch, to the law.

He was familiar with the south-east corner of Indian Territory, and he decided to hide out for a while in a small ravine eleven miles north of the Red River, where he had stayed once before with his men.

He crossed the river, then headed north-west. After riding a few miles, it occured to him that it might be advisable for him to make things difficult for anyone who could be trailing him.

Taking care to ride over ground which made his tracks difficult to follow, he rode on for a further five miles, then veered to the north, in the direction of the ravine. He now took particular care to hide his tracks, dismounting now and again to obliterate them with a piece of brush. On reaching the ravine, he decided to stay there for a few days, considering his next move.

When the brothers had forded the Red, on the day after Taylor's arrival at the ravine, and had headed north-west on his trail, Jimmy soon realized that the outlaw was doing his best to hide his tracks.

When they reached a point about eight miles from the ford, he was convinced that Taylor had, somewhere near that point, left the trail along which they were riding. He asked his brothers to wait while he rode in a wide circle to see if he could spot the hoof-prints of Taylor's horse.

While doing this, he was riding down a steep slope studded with embedded pieces of rock, and covered in parts with loose stones, when the ground suddenly gave way under his horse's hoofs. The horse lost its footing.

Jimmy was thrown sideways from the saddle, and his horse, struggling to regain its footing, stamped on his right leg before Jimmy rolled down the slope and came up against a large boulder which lay in his path. As his body hit the boulder, his head slammed against it, and he lay there, stunned. The horse, which had regained its footing, appeared to be unharmed.

Danny and Jack both witnessed the fall from a distance, and they rode quickly to help their brother.

As they reached him, his eyes opened and he looked around.

'Is my horse all right?' he asked.

Jack walked over and examined the animal.

'Looks all right, Jimmy,' he replied.

There was a nasty gash on Jimmy's temple, which was bleeding. Danny put a pad over the wound, and held it in place with a bandage around his head. Then he started to help Jimmy to rise to his feet.

As soon as the weight came on to his right leg, Jimmy shouted with pain, and sank back to the ground. Danny examined the leg. It was badly bruised just above the knee, and it seemed that the knee had been badly twisted.

'We need to find a doctor,' said Danny. 'Maybe there's one in that town Briscoe that Wilkin told us about. I reckon it's only six miles or so ahead. We'll go there.'

'I'm sorry,' said Jimmy. 'That was a fool thing to do, and just when we were getting near to Taylor again.'

'Jimmy,' said Danny, 'Jack and me, we both know you're a darned sight better rider than either of us. That was just plain bad luck, your horse going down like that. And as for Taylor, he can wait.'

Danny carried Jimmy to the top of the slope, then lifted him on to his horse. When they arrived at Briscoe, and enquired about a doctor, they were directed to the house of Doc Bannister, next door to the livery stable.

Bannister was at home, and when Danny knocked on the door he invited them in. He was a small, middle-aged man, with keen eyes in a round, pleas-ant face, He examined Jimmy's head, then cleaned the wound and replaced the pad and bandage with clean ones.

'Should heal up all right,' he said, then turned his attention to the leg.

'The knee's been badly wrenched,' he said, when he had examined it. 'The only thing I can recom-mend for that is rest.'

'How long will it take?' asked Danny.

'Four or five days,' Bannister replied. 'And I *mean* rest. No walking or riding.'

They thanked the doctor, then took a room at the hotel along the street.

Three days after Jimmy's mishap, Taylor decided to ride into Elkin, a small town six miles north of the ravine, for provisions. As he rode into town, he saw a freight wagon, with a team of six mules, standing outside the general store. The driver and owner of the wagon, Josh Turnbull, was standing on the board-walk and a small crowd had collected in front of him.

Turnbull was a weather-beaten veteran of the Indian Wars, still hale and hearty in his late sixties. Driving his freight wagon, he made frequent trips from Texas to Indian Territory. As well as delivering freight, he performed another useful function as a dispenser of news to communities starved in that respect.

With only the company of his mules over long periods of time, he welcomed the chance of speaking to his fellow men; and it was his practice, after making a delivery, to pass on to the assembled crowd news of any eventful happenings which had come to his notice along the way.

Taylor tied his horse to a hitching rail and walked over to the back of the crowd as Turnbull began to speak.

'There's one main item of news today, folks,' he said, 'and it sure is a humdinger. I got it from Wilkin, the liveryman in Langtry on the other side of the Red. Seems like the Box D horse ranch near there has been run for a long time by a man called Devlin as a hideout for outlaws on the run.

'This was found out by three young brothers called Brannigan, who were chasing a man called Taylor, who was the killer of their father Joe Brannigan. The eldest of the boys is only eighteen. Joe had been a Texas Ranger, and he put Taylor in the penitentiary about eight years ago.

'The boys followed Taylor to the Box D, and two of them were captured by Devlin, but the youngest managed to free them and they told the Rangers about Devlin's operation. Taylor escaped, and the brothers are now looking for him in Indian Territory. I sure hope they find him.'

As Turnbull continued with some less important news items, Taylor, badly shaken by the news that Danny and Jack had escaped from Devlin, hurried to the store and bought the supplies he needed. Then he rode back to the ravine, and reviewed the situation.

He now knew the identities of Danny and Jack, both of whom he had met. He also now knew why they, with their brother, were after him. Despite their youth, it seemed that they presented a real threat to him. He decided that he badly needed help.

While in prison he had heard of a gang of three men, Starkey, Bishop and Lassiter, whose guns were for hire for any illegal operation, including murder. Taylor had been interested at the time because he had thought of hiring them to kill Joe Brannigan. But he later decided that he wanted the satisfaction of doing this himself.

The man in prison, who had once hired the gang for his own purposes, had told Taylor that the way to get in touch with the leader, Starkey, was to ride to Tapita, a small settlement in Indian Territory, where there was a store, saloon and boarding-house.

'Go into the saloon,' the man had said, 'and mention to the barkeep that you'd like to talk to Starkey. If he *is* around, and decides he wants to see you, *he*'ll come to you.'

It so happened that Tapita was only around twelve miles away to the north-west, and Taylor decided to ride there immediately. On arrival, he went into the saloon. Apart from the barkeep, a small man with a drooping moustache, the saloon was empty. He asked for a beer and when it was passed to him he said he would like to talk to Starkey.

The barkeep studied him closely.

'Is it a matter of business?' he asked.

'That's right,' Taylor replied.

'You'd better book a room at the boarding-house,' said the barkeep. 'If he figures he wants to talk with you, likely it won't be till tomorrow.'

'I'll do that,' said Taylor.

Quickly, he finished his beer, then went along to his room at the boarding-house, where, apart from leaving for meals, he stayed for the rest of the day.

As he was finishing breakfast the following morning, the barkeep came in and asked him to follow him outside. He pointed to an old tumbledown, deserted shack on the edge of town.

'Starkey'll see you behind that shack in thirty minutes,' he said.

When Taylor reached the shack half an hour later, two men were standing behind it. Their horses were nearby. One of the men was dressed in black. He was of average height and clean-shaven, with a bleak, angular face. He scrutinized Taylor closely.

'Starkey?' asked Taylor.

The man nodded. 'Who told you about finding me here?' he asked abruptly. His voice was harsh.

Taylor explained how his fellow prisoner had told him how to make contact. He named the prisoner.

'You got a proposition for me?' asked Starkey.

'I have,' said Taylor, and proceeded to tell Starkey about his pursuit by the Brannigan brothers: what had led up to it; the loss of the other two members of his gang; and the exposure of Devlin's Box D operation in aid of criminals.

'I know for a fact,' he went on, 'that those three are still after me. I want you to finish them off for good.'

'That shouldn't be too hard,' said Starkey. 'Sounds like they ain't hardly growed up yet. Maybe they've just been lucky up to now.'

'I ain't so sure about that,' said Taylor.

'That name "Brannigan",' said Starkey, ignoring Taylor's remark. 'I think I heard Lassiter here mention the name yesterday when he was talking to my other man Bishop. What was it, Lassiter, that you were telling Bishop?'

Lassiter, a rangy sandy-haired man, who walked with a slight limp, told them that when he was in Briscoe, about fifteen miles distant, on the previous day, he heard some talk about three brothers called Brannigan who were in town, chasing a man called Taylor who had killed their father. They'd been asking if Taylor had been seen in the area.

It seemed, Lassiter said, that the youngest of the three, a boy of sixteen, had taken a fall off his horse and his head and leg had been damaged. So the three were staying on in Briscoe for a few days.

'So,' said Starkey to Taylor, 'we know exactly where they are, for a day or two at least. That makes things easier for us. But I don't want to take them in town, with folks looking on. We'll think up some way of setting a trap for them, outside of town.

'Meanwhile, you'd better stay at our hideout till the job's finished. It's in a ravine three miles north of here. We're using an old deserted cabin that somebody built there.'

Starkey and Taylor reached agreement over the payment to be handed over for the triple murder. Then all three left town, heading for the hideout.

The ravine was narrow and secluded, well away from any of the main trails in the area. When they arrived, Bishop walked· out of the cabin as they dismounted. He looked curiously at Taylor. Seeing the three of them together, Taylor felt a sudden chill. They all had the same bleak, merciless look about them.

Starkey introduced Bishop to Taylor, and briefly explained to him the nature of the job the gang were to undertake for him. Then he turned to Lassiter.

'Ride into Briscoe,' he said, 'and find out when that young Brannigan boy's going to be fit to ride again. Then come back and let me know.'

Lassiter rode off, and Taylor listened as Starkey and Bishop discussed a plan for dealing with the three brothers. Lassiter returned after dark to report that the doctor had cleared the injured Brannigan boy as fit to ride the day after next, and that the three brothers intended to leave town on the morning of that day to resume the search for Taylor.

'Good,' said Starkey, then went over with Lassiter the plan he had discussed with Bishop.

The following day, keeping well off the main trail, Lassiter rode Taylor's horse to Briscoe, arriving there just as darkness was falling. He tethered the horse on the edge of town, then went in search of the brothers, who were in their room at the hotel. He knocked on the door, and Jack let him in.

Trying to assume a pleasant look, which didn't sit too easily on his bleak face, Lassiter told them that he was in the area on business, and had heard about their search for an outlaw called Taylor.

He said that earlier in the day he had been riding from Tapita to Briscoe, and about half-way along the trail had passed a rider moving in the opposite direction. The man hadn't seemed inclined to stop and talk, but had passed on with a wave of the hand.

'A bit later on,' said Lassiter, 'it hit me that he might be the man you're after, but I ain't too sure what Taylor looks like. Is he a big man, with a scar on his left cheek?'

'That's right,' said Danny. 'What sort of horse was he riding?'

'A big chestnut,' Lassiter replied, 'with a white stripe down its face.'

'That sure sounds like him,' said Danny. 'We'll ride out on the Tapita trail in the morning, and see if we can pick up his tracks.'

'Somebody was telling me,' said Lassiter, 'that one of you is a pretty good tracker, so maybe you'll be able to catch up with this man Taylor.'

'We sure hope so,' said Danny. 'We're obliged for what you just told us.'

Lassiter returned to Taylor's horse and rode back towards Tapita, keeping well off the main trail before joining it about six miles out of Briscoe. He stayed on the trail for four miles, then branched off to the left and headed for a secluded box canyon, familiar to him, three miles ahead. The canyon, sheer-sided, with only one way in or out, was to play an important role in the plan for the disposal of the Brannigan brothers.

When he reached the entrance to the canyon, Lassiter was sure that a tracker of average ability would be able to follow the tracks of the horse he was riding, from the point where he had joined the Briscoe – Tapita trail, right up to the box canyon.

He rode into the canyon and stopped half-way along it, outside the entrance to a cave stretching back from the sheer wall. He tethered the horse, took some food and drink which he had brought with him, and settled down for the rest of the night.

Starkey and Bishop rode off early in the morning, leaving Taylor in the ravine. They arrived at the box canyon, where Lassiter awaited them, at daybreak, having approached it from the end opposite to the entrance. They rode along the rim until they could see Lassiter standing outside the cave.

He spotted them and waved. Then, leaving the horse behind, he took a broom he had brought with him and slowly walked backwards to the canyon entrance, removing all trace of his own footprints. He continued to do this as he climbed up to the canyon rim to join Starkey and Bishop.

All three headed for a tall rocky outcrop, not far from the canyon rim, and tethered the two horses behind it. Then they climbed to the top, from which they had a clear view of the mouth of the cave and the entrance to the canyon. The top of the outcrop was covered with a jumble of large boulders, and the three men each selected a position from which he could fire from cover towards the canyon below. Then they settled down to wait.

'When those three reach the canyon entrance,' said Starkey, and they see the horse, and only a set of horse-tracks leading in, they're bound to reckon that Taylor's in the cave. And they'll have no reason to think that there's anybody else around. I figure that if there's no sign of anybody watching them from inside the cave, they'll run around the wall till they reach it.

'We'll open up on them when they're getting near. They'll be in rifle range by then. They'll be sitting ducks. There ain't nowhere for them to take cover.'

TWELVE

The Brannigan brothers left Briscoe at about the same time as Starkey and Bishop arrived at the canyon. They rode along the trail towards Tapita, and after they had covered about six miles, Jimmy caught his first sight of the tracks of Taylor's horse.

They lost the tracks four miles further on, but doubling back a short distance, Jimmy found that Taylor's horse had left the trail to Tapita, and had headed in a westterly direction.

Following the tracks, they eventually reached the canyon entrance, through which the tracks continued. They dismounted at one side of the entrance, and Danny peered into the canyon. He saw the mouth of the cave, and the chestnut horse standing nearby. There was no sign of Taylor himself. He retreated, and told the others what he had seen.

A moment later, Jimmy, studying the tracks at the canyon entrance, could see only those left by Taylor's horse. 'Let's go in,' said Jack. 'We've got him cornered. It shouldn't be too hard to capture him now.'

Danny nodded, and they tethered their horses against a patch of brush not visible from inside the canyon. With each of the three armed with a six-gun and rifle, Danny started to lead the way into the canyon. Then he hesitated, and stopped.

'It sure looks like Taylor's in there on his own,' he said, 'but compared with all the trouble we've had chasing him since we left home, finding him here's been pretty easy. Maybe we're riding into a trap. Or maybe I'm worrying when there's no need.

'All the same, I'm going to feel better, Jack, if you move around the rim of the canyon, and stop about half-way between here and the cave. I noticed some big boulders standing there, close to the top of the wall, that'll give you cover. We're going to feel a lot better inside the canyon with a sharpshooter like you up there.

'Keep an eye out for any movement outside the canyon, and Jimmy and me'll run to the cave to see if Taylor's inside. We'll keep a little way clear of the wall, so's you'll be able to see us. We'll give you twenty minutes to get into position, before we go into the canyon.'

When Jack reached the group of boulders at the top of the canyon wall, he could see that they were ideal for cover. From behind one of them, close to the edge, he had a good view down into the canyon. He settled down to wait for Jimmy and Jack to appear at the canyon entrance.

Starkey and his men, concealed on top of the outcrop, had seen the three brothers approaching the canyon when they were still some distance away. They passed out of view as they approached the canyon entrance, and the next movement that Starkey and the others observed came some time later, when Jack appeared at the top of the canyon wall, and took cover among the boulders.

'Damnation!' shouted Starkey, seeing his carefully laid plan go somewhat awry. 'Forget about the man at the top of the wall for now. I reckon he's too far away for accurate rifle-shooting.

'I figure the other two'll be moving into the canyon any time now. I reckon they'll be inside rifle range by the time they're getting near the cave. When I give the say-so, we'll all fire at them. We should be able to nail them good. Then we'll tend to the other one.'

Waiting for Danny and Jimmy to appear in view, Jack checked the lever-action Winchester .44 – .40 rifle, with extra rear sight, which was his pride and joy. He saw them enter the canyon, both holding their rifles. Staring ahead of them, they ran side by side, parallel to the canyon wall, a few yards away from it.

They were nearing the cave entrance when Danny suddenly doubled up and fell to the ground. A moment later, there was the sound of a rifle shot coming from the far side of the canyon. Jimmy heard the shot, looked back, and saw that his brother had gone down.

As he ran back to Danny, two bullets narrowly missed him, and struck the bottom of the canyon wall. He crouched down to shield his brother, but with no cover available, it seemed only a matter of time before he was hit.

As Jack saw Danny go down, and heard the rifle shot, he looked across the canyon and saw gunsmoke at the top of the outcrop. He also caught a glimpse of moving figures.

He steadied himself, acutely aware that the lives off his brothers could well depend on his swift and effective action. He had noticed earlier that a slight breeze was coming from behind him.

He quickly adjusted the rear sight on the Winchester, and took careful aim at what looked like the head and shoulders of a man lying on top of the outcrop, firing a rifle down into the canyon. The rest of the man's body was hidden behind a boulder.

Jack pulled the trigger. As the bullet entered Bishop's head, he dropped his rifle and slumped on the ground. Moments later, as the shocked Starkey was bending over to look at the dead man at his feet, he himself was struck in the chest, below the right shoulder, by the second bullet from Jack's Winchester.

Lassiter, a few yards away, stopped firing at Jimmy, crawled over to Starkey, who had fallen on top of Bishop, and dragged him behind the boulder. He could see that Bishop was dead.

Down in the canyon, Jimmy, who had survived two more near misses, heard the two shots from Jack, after which there was silence. Underneath him, he saw, with relief, that Danny, who had heard the two shots from Jack, was getting to his feet. In the absence of gunfire from the cave, Danny was sure now that it was empty.

'Run for the cave, Jimmy,' he said. 'I'm all right. I'll be right behind you.

Jimmy sprinted for the cave, and Danny, bent almost double, and moving more slowly, followed him inside. At the back of the cave, safe from any fire from the outcrop, Danny, with the aid of matches, which Jimmy struck and held for him, examined his wound.

He discovered that the rifle bullet had struck the heavy metal buckle of his belt, and had driven it with considerable force against the flesh beneath. The result was severe bruising of the flesh underneath the belt, but no serious damage appeared to have been done.

Jack saw Jimmy run into the cave, followed by Danny. He wondered how badly Danny was hurt. He looked towards the outcrop again. A single rifle was being fired in his direction from the side of one of the boulders. But the bullets were passing nowhere near him.

He took careful aim at the rifleman, and fired. Lassiter, on the point of firing, cursed as Jack's bullet passed within an inch of his right ear. He decided to remain behind the boulder and discuss the situation with Starkey, who was suffering from shock and the pain from the bullet wound in his chest.

'With a rifleman like that down there,' said Starkey, 'we're stuck here till after dark. There's only one way we can climb down, and that's in his view. We'll leave as soon as it's too dark for him to see us. Meanwhile, send a shot into the mouth of that cave now and again. But mind you keep out of sight of that sharpshooter.'

Jack also, had decided that he had better stay put until it was dark, before going to find out how badly Danny was injured.

As soon as darkness eventually came, and accurate rifle shooting was impossible, Lassiter helped Starkey down to the foot of the outcrop. As they reached the bottom, Starkey, groaning with pain, fell to his knees. Lassiter helped him to his feet, and they walked slowly round the outcrop to the horses. The dead body of Bishop had been left behind.

'We'll go back to the hideout,' said Starkey, weakly, 'and seeing as you know the country pretty well around here, take a route that won't show any tracks for them to follow.

'When we get back to the cabin, I'm going to get you to have a go at digging this bullet out. I've got a feeling it ain't in too deep.

'Then we've get to think up some way of finishing off those three Brannigans. It's personal now that they plugged me and killed Bishop. I never figured we'd have this much trouble with teen-agers like that.'

Jack left his cover at about the same time as Starkey and Lassiter. Cautiously, he worked his way down to the canyon entrance, pausing to listen now and again. He entered the canyon and walked along the wall towards the mouth of the cave. Just before reaching it, he stopped and called out.

'You there, Danny?' he asked. 'It's Jack here.'

'Figured you'd be along soon,' said Danny, appearing in the cave entrance with Jimmy by his side. He was standing in a slightly bent position, his hands clasping his stomach.

'You got hit, Danny?' asked Jack.

'I had a stroke of luck,' Danny replied. 'The bullet that hit me was stopped by the buckle on my belt. I've got a belly that's mighty sore, but I don't figure any real harm's been done. It sure was lucky for us, you being on look-out up there.'

'That was *your* doing,' said Jack. 'As for the men on the outcrop, I ain't dead certain, but I think there were three of them. And I reckon that maybe I hit two.'

'I'm wondering just who they are,' said Danny. 'I reckon Taylor's called in some help. D'you think they've left the outcrop by now?'

'It depends,' said Jack. 'If they can still walk, they'd be crazy to stay up there.'

'Right,' said Danny, 'We'll stay here in the cave for the rest of the night, with a guard on the entrance. Come morning, we'll ride up to the outcrop and have a look round there.'

When daylight came, they could see no sign of men on top of the outcrop. They went for their horses, Danny wincing with pain as he mounted. They rode up to the outcrop, taking Taylor's horse with them.

Jack and Jimmy climbed to the top and rejoined Danny fifteen minutes later.

'There's a dead man up there,' said Jack, 'with a bullet in the head. He's a stranger to us. And there's a fair amount of blood on the ground. Jimmy reckons there were three men up there, and one of the two who left was wounded. There's plenty of loose stones up there. D'you reckon we should cover that body?'

'Yes,' said Danny.

When they had finished the job, Jimmy started looking for tracks which they could follow. But soon he had to admit defeat.

'Those two,' he said, 'have done too good a job of hiding their tracks. I'm just going to be wasting time looking for them.'

'Right,' said Danny. 'What's the nearest town?'

'Must be Tapita,' Jack replied.

'We'll head there, then,' said Danny, 'and start nosing around. If one of the men's badly wounded, he'll have to rest up somewhere around here. And maybe we can find out something about that man, Lassiter, who told us about seeing Taylor between Briscoe and Tapita.'

They rode on to Tapita, and took a room in the boarding-house, which was run by a pleasant widowed lady, Mrs Curtis, who had a young son called Johnny, aged eight.

Danny lay on the bed until supper-time, and the pain under his belt began to ease off. After supper, the brothers went back to their room to discuss their next move. Danny lay down on the bed again.

'The only lead we've got now is that man Lassiter,' he said. 'It seems clear that he was working for Taylor. Maybe he was one of the men on the outcrop. If only we could locate him, maybe he would lead us to Taylor.

'Go and see Mrs Curtis, Jack, and see if she knows anything about Lassiter.'

Jack found Mrs Curtis sitting in her living-room with Johnny. He described Lassiter in detail, and said that it was important that he and his brothers located the man. He asked her if she had seen him around.

'I can't say that I have,' she said. ' I think I'd have remembered him. I'm sorry.'

'I've seen him,' said Johnny. 'Two days ago I was playing hide-and-seek with Bill Tyler near that old empty shack on the edge of town, and I saw him talking with two other men. I only saw the backs of the other two, but I got a good look at the man you were talking about. And I saw him limping when he was walking over to his horse.'

'Thanks, Johnny,' said Jack. 'Maybe what you've told us is going to help us a lot. If you happen to see the man again while we're here, let us know. He's a bad man, and we aim to see that he's handed over to the law. Don't speak to him. Just let us know you've seen him. Is that all right with you, Mrs Curtis?'

'Of course,' she replied. 'But remember, Johnny, don't talk to the man, and don't act like you're spying on him.'

When Jack returned to his brothers, he told them about Johnny seeing Lassiter in town.

'Maybe,' said Danny, 'Lassiter has an accomplice here in town. Let's put out a story that we're leaving this area. If Lassiter and the men on the outcrop are still around, it'll put them off their guard. The best man to tell the story to first is the barkeep. Tell him, and the news'll soon get around town.

'Better do it now, Jack. Go in for a drink. Say that we got a report from a rider we met on the trail, that he spotted a man riding into Grady, that's sixty miles west of here, who might be the one that we're after. Say that we're riding there just as soon as I'm fit.'

When Starkey and Lassiter arrived back at the ravine, Taylor, who was lying down in the cabin, heard them outside. He rose, picked up his revolver, and waited until he heard Lassiter's voice telling him to light a lamp and let them in.

As the two men came in, Taylor saw that Lassiter was half-supporting Starkey, who was holding a bloodstained bandanna against a wound on his chest, below the right shoulder. Alarmed at the sight, Taylor held the door open, expecting Bishop to come in. When he failed to appear, Taylor looked outside. There was no sign of the third member of the gang. He closed the door.

Starkey was lying on one of the beds, and Lassiter was removing the wounded man's vest and shirt. Taylor put some wood on the stove, then put some water on to heat up. He could see that Starkey was in an evil mood, and that this wasn't the right time for questions.

Lassiter heated the most suitable knife he could find for the job, and probed for the bullet. As Starkey had thought, it had not penetrated deeply, and Lassiter was soon able to dig it out, to the accompaniment of a volley of groans and curses from the patient.

Lassiter then cleaned the wound as best he could,

placed a pad over it, and applied a bandage to hold it in position. When he had finished, the supply of bandage held in the cabin was completely exhausted.

'If this ain't going to get infected,' said Starkey to Lassiter, 'we need a lot more clean bandages. You'd better ride into Tapita for some tomorrow morning, and bring some whiskey as well. Don't let anybody but the barkeep see you. Go into the saloon through the back door, and get the barkeep to get the bandages from the store for you. And ask him if anybody knows where the Brannigan brothers are right now.'

Taylor had waited with mounting impatience to hear how Starkey had come to be wounded, and what had happened to Bishop. Starkey now enlightened him.

'That job you hired us for,' he said, 'didn't turn out as easy as I figured it would be. One of the three turned out to be one of the best long-range rifle shots I've ever come up against. He killed Bishop with his first shot and hit me with his second. And we'd figured he was too far away for accurate rifle-shooting.

'And another one, probably the one who's leading them, is a thinker. What I mean is, he don't jump in without thinking. And that's what saved the three of them.'

'All three are still alive, then?' said Taylor.

Starkey nodded. 'One of them was hit,' he said, 'but it wasn't bad enough to stop him running for cover.'

'I think I'll be moving on tomorrow,' said Taylor,

'but I'll hang around till Lassiter gets back from Tapita, in case he has any news of the Brannigans. I don't feel safe here with those three still on the loose, with you wounded, and only the two of you left. I'm cancelling the contract, but you can keep the down payment I made.'

Starkey scowled. 'Suit yourself,' he said. 'This is personal now. Bishop and Lassiter and me, we've been together a long time. As soon as I'm fit, Lassiter and me are going after those three, and this time we won't make no mistakes.'

THIRTEEN

On the following morning, Lassiter rode towards the deserted shack in Tapita outside which he and Starkey had first met Taylor. Inside the shack, Johnny Curtis, playing with his friend Billy Tyler, which was something they did in the shack occasionally, saw Lassiter approaching.

He signalled to Billy to be quiet, and the two boys watched through gaps in the walls as Lassiter tethered his horse behind the shack, then walked along the backs of the buildings and entered the rear door of the saloon.

As soon as Lassiter had disappeared from view, the two boys left the shack, and Johnny ran to the room in the boarding-house to which Danny and his brothers had returned after breakfast. Breathlessly, he told them that Lassiter had just gone into the saloon through the back door.

'He must be in cahoots with the barkeep,' said Danny.

He asked Jimmy to go somewhere where he could hide and watch Lassiter's horse, so that he could come back and tell them when Lassiter left town.

When Lassiter went into the saloon, which was empty of customers, he asked the barkeep if three brothers called Brannigan had turned up in town. He was told that they were staying in the boarding-house, and that one of them had told the barkeep that the man they were chasing might be one that was seen near Grady, and that all three of them were leaving for Grady as soon as one of them, who had been injured, was fit.

The barkeep then went to the store for the bandages. When he returned with them, he checked that the coast was clear. Lassiter, carrying the bandages and some whiskey, returned to his horse and rode off, confident that no one but the barkeep had been aware of his presence in town.

Jimmy ran back with the news that Lassiter was leaving, heading north, and the three brothers, Danny feeling better after a night's rest, went for their horses and rode to the edge of town.

'You go first, Jimmy,' said Danny. 'He ain't so likely to spot only one rider. We'll follow you. We'll keep in sight, and you wave to us to ride on when it's safe.'

Lassiter showed no sign of suspecting that he might be followed, and they had trailed him for three miles, when Jimmy saw him disappear into a small ravine. From cover, he watched for a while, but Lassiter did not reappear. He waved to his brothers, who rode up to join him. Jimmy pointed to the ravine.

'He rode in there,' he said, 'and he ain't come out.'

'We've got to take a look inside there without being seen,' said Danny, looking over at the ravine, and seeing the group of trees on the high ground bordering its near side. 'We'll swing round from here, and ride straight into that grove. From inside it, we should be able to look down into the ravine.'

They rode into the grove, dismounted, then walked to where the grove petered out at the top of the slope leading down into the ravine. They lay on the ground, and looked at the scene below.

They saw a cabin, which had obviously been standing there for many years. Three horses were grazing nearby, and a wisp of smoke was coming from the chimney pipe projecting through the roof of the cabin. They watched for a while, but the door of the cabin remained closed.

'It looks like there may be three men inside there,' said Danny, 'and maybe one of them's Taylor. I reckon the best plan for us is to go back to Tapita and come back here after dark, so's we can get up to the cabin without being seen. That way, maybe we can take them without too much blood being shed.'

They walked back to their horses and returned to Tapita.

When Lassiter had joined Starkey and Taylor in the cabin after his visit to Tapita, he told them of the presence of the Brannigans in town, and of their intention to investigate a reported sighting of Taylor near Grady. It was then that Taylor took a decision.

'I'll be leaving as soon as it's dark,' he said, 'and I've a notion to take a shotgun with me.'

He pointed to a double-barrelled Remington 10-gauge shotgun, with shortened barrels, which was hanging on the wall.

'I'd like to trade my Winchester .44 for the shotgun,' he said. 'Is it a deal?'

Starkey looked at him curiously.

'That shotgun belonged to Bishop,' he said. 'You can take it. There's some ammunition on the shelf beside it.'

Taylor rode off at dusk, on Bishop's horse, heading for Tapita. He dismounted just outside town and stood by his mount while he loaded both barrels of the shotgun. Then, holding the gun, he walked along the deserted street in the shadows.

When he saw the building with the BOARDING-HOUSE sign, he slipped around to the back and found a window belonging to the dining-room. Cautiously looking inside, he saw three young men seated along one side of a large table, taking a meal.

All three were facing Taylor, and there was nobody else in the room. Immediately, he recognized Danny and Jack. The third one, younger than the others, he assumed to be their brother.

As he continued to watch, the meal came to an end, and Mrs Curtis appeared and started to clear the table. Then the three brothers rose from the table and left the room. In view of the recent attempt on their lives, they were all wearing their six-guns.

Shortly after they left the room, a light shone out of a window further along the rear wall of the building, as a lamp was lit inside a room. A curtain was drawn across the window just before Taylor reached it.

Inside the room, Jack realized that he had not mentioned to Mrs Curtis that they would all be going out later that night. He walked back to the kitchen to tell her so.

Taylor stood outside the window for a short while, then he walked back along the wall, counting the windows, until he reached a door. Carefully, he turned the handle, and opened it. It led into a passage lit by an oil-lamp. He closed the door behind him and tiptoed along the passage until he came, on his left, to another well-lit passage leading to the bedroom doors.

He tiptoed along the carpeted floor of this passage, counting the doors as he passed them until, at the end of the passage, he reached the door of the room occupied by the Brannigans. Inside, Jimmy and Jack had both taken off their gunbelts and had hung them on the back of a chair in the corner of the room.

As Taylor cocked the two triggers on his shotgun, he looked at the door, which had been left slightly ajar by Danny on his way out. He placed the ends of the shotgun barrels against the door, preparatory to pushing it wide open to reveal the occupants for whom the two lethal loads of buckshot were intended.

At that precise moment, Danny, walking silently along the carpeted floor, turned into the passage and recognized Taylor, and the danger to his brothers from the deadly weapon in his hand. His reaction

151

was immediate. Just as the door started to open, Danny drew his Peacemaker with a rapidity born of desperation, and shot Taylor in the head.

Taylor's finger slipped away from the trigger without pressing it, but as the shotgun fell and hit the floor, a hammer fell, and a barrel discharged. Fortunately, the buckshot load slammed harmlessly into the wall at the end of the passage.

At the sound of gunfire, Jack ran for his revolver, then headed for the door. As he did so, it opened wide under the pressure of Taylor's body, and the dead outlaw slumped on the floor, half inside the room. Jack and Jimmy stared down at the man whose trail they had followed for so long.

Then, to their relief, Danny spoke to them from outside the door. He told them what had happened.

Mrs Curtis came running from the kitchen, and when she had recovered from the shock of seeing the dead man, Danny explained to her that he was the outlaw for whom they had long been searching, who had murdered their father. He asked her if there was an undertaker in town who would take care of the body.

'Yes,' she said. 'Fred White'll see to it. I'll go for him now.'

'I'll see that the law hears about this when I get the chance,' said Danny.

'We have a couple of deputy US marshals calling here every now and then,' she said. 'They should be showing up any time now.'

'That's good,' said Danny. 'Now, you remember me telling you a few minutes ago that we were leaving town for a while later tonight. We'll still be going. This man here had hired some people to help him kill the three of us. We're going to pay them a visit tonight. Then we'll come back here.'

'All right,' she said. 'I'll go for Fred White now.'

White came soon after, and took the body away. Then the brothers helped Mrs Curtis to clean up the mess. Danny offered to pay for repairs to the damage caused by the shotgun blast.

At half an hour before midnight, the brothers left Tapita for Starkey's hideout. They left their horses outside the ravine, and Jimmy went in on foot to check that no guard had been stationed outside the cabin; to have a close look at the cabin itself; and to check on some points raised by Danny. He returned twenty minutes later.

'There's nobody outside the cabin,' he reported, 'There are two horses there now, instead of the three we saw earlier. There's a lamp burning inside, and the windows are covered over. But there's a few narrow gaps in the wall timbers, and I could see two men.

'One of them was lying on a bed, with a wound in his chest, and a shotgun on the table by him. The other man was Lassiter. He was starting to take the bandages off the wound. I couldn't see anybody else there.'

'Did you see if the door's fastened on the inside?' asked Danny.

'Yes,' replied Jimmy. 'There's a bar across it. But it don't look all that strong.'

'Did you see a heavy piece of timber we could use

to ram that door?' asked Danny.

'Yes,' Jimmy replied. 'There's a length of old tree-trunk lying half-buried in the grass near the cabin. I think that would do.'

'We'd better get moving then,' said Danny. 'We need to bust in there before the lamp's put out.'

They hurried into the ravine, and freed the trunk. Then Jimmy and Danny crept up to the cabin, and Danny looked inside, through the gaps in the walls. He saw Lassiter applying a clean bandage to the man on the bed. Then he looked at the shotgun and the door-fastening, before returning with Jimmy to where Jack was waiting by the piece of tree-trunk.

The three of them lifted the heavy piece of timber and carried it further away from the cabin, to a point where they were exactly opposite the door.

'This should do,' said Danny. 'We'll aim at the middle of the door, and work up as much speed as we can before we hit it.'

Inside the cabin, Lassiter was just fastening off the bandage around Starkey's chest, when both men looked towards the door as they heard a sound outside.

Immediately after this, the door burst open and fell to the floor, with the length of trunk on top of it. The three brothers ran inside. Danny made for Starkey, picking the shotgun off the table as the wounded man was reaching for it with his left hand. He jammed the muzzle of his own revolver into the side of Starkey's neck.

Jack ran up towards Lassiter as he was moving towards his gunbelt hanging on the wall. Lassiter froze as he felt the muzzle of Jack's six-gun against his back. Minutes later, his hands and feet had been bound, and he was sitting on the floor, against the wall. Starkey was lying on the bed, with his feet tied, and his left hand secured to the bed.

Danny looked at the pair with some satisfaction.

'All we have to do now,' he said, 'is hand these two over to the law, then we can all go home.'

Sullenly, Starkey and Lassiter regarded their youthful captors. After the numerous successful operations, most involving murder, which they had completed in the past, their complete and humiliating defeat by the three brothers was entirely unexpected.

When daylight came, Danny asked Jimmy to ride into Tapita, and ask the storekeeper how they could get in touch with the law, to arrange for Starkey and Lassiter to be picked up.

When Jimmy reached town, he put the question to the storekeeper, who was just about to reply when, through the store window, he saw two riders coming into town from the east.

'You're lucky,' he said, pointing to the riders. 'I was just going to say that we'd likely have a couple of US marshals calling in later in the week. They're the ones.'

He went out on to the boardwalk with Jimmy, and called the two riders, Bond and Garner, over. He introduced Jimmy, who told them about the shooting of Taylor, the capture of Lassiter and his partner, and the death of another man near the canyon.

'Looks like you and your brothers have been

pretty busy,' said Garner. 'You mentioned the name Lassiter. There's a Lassiter in the Starkey gang, as well as Starkey himself, and a man called Bishop. Leaving out the man Taylor, tell me what the other three look like.'

The deputies listened, with mounting interest, as Jimmy described the three men.

'You've just described the Starkey gang,' said Garner. 'It's the gang we've been after for years, but we've never been able to get our hands on them. We're going with you right now to that ravine where your brothers are holding them.'

When Jimmy and the deputies reached the cabin, the prisoners were handed over to the lawmen, who confirmed the identities of Starkey and Lassiter. Danny told them exactly where Bishop had been buried. Then the brothers returned to Tapita.

After a meal at the boarding-house, they sat in their room, more relaxed than they had been for a long time.

'I'm going out now to arrange for a message to be sent to Mr Parker on the Circle Dot, telling him what's happened here,' said Danny. 'And tomorrow morning, we'll hit the trail for the Lazy B. We've got a ranch to run.'